Praise for Cassandra Dean

Cassandra Dean spins a story where this reader could share in the ache, and desire, that embraces the characters and brings out true emotion.
–The Romance Studio

It takes a special kind of talent to craft a compelling [sic] story–it takes very unique talent indeed to create characters as engaging and sympathetic as those found in Cassandra Dean's stories.
–The Romance Reviews

With just a whisper, a caress, or a simple kiss, Ms. Dean takes the reader on an adventure full of hedonistic pleasure as well as bittersweet moments.
– Coffee Time Romance

Silk & Scars

THE SILK SERIES BOOK 3

Cassandra Dean

By Cassandra Dean

Enslaved
Teach Me
Scandalous
Rough Diamond
Fool's Gold
Emerald Sea
Silk & Scandal
Silk & Scorn
Silk & Scars
Silk & Scholar
Silk & Scarlet
Slumber
Awaken
Finding Lord Farlisle
Rescuing Lord Roxwaithe
Stealing Lord Stephen
Persuading Lady Penelope

Dedication

To everyone who helped along the way.

Silk & Scars

The Silk Series Book 3

Cassandra Dean

Prologue

Beecham & Co Chambers, London, 17 March 1845

To His Grace, the Duke of Sowrith,

Your Grace,
Please find enclosed the most recent version of your Last Will and Testament as well as your Enduring Power of Attorney. Please note your request to establish lines of inheritance regarding a potential beneficiary in foreign nations is being undertaken. A report will be produced and enclosed in our next correspondence.
Yours, etc.
Lord Peter Beecham
Solicitor

***

Sowrithil, Devon, 27 December 1845

Lord Beecham,
A redraft of my Will and Testament is required.

A separate missive will be sent detailing who the new beneficiaries are and what they will receive.
 Signed
 His Grace, the Duke of Sowrith

***

Beecham & Co Chambers, London, 23 May 1846

To His Grace, the Duke of Sowrith,

Your Grace,
 We have received your request to update your Will and holdings to your Estate. We will be in correspondence if we require any further information.
 Please note we have found a potential claimant to your Estate in Wyoming Territory in the Americas. We anticipate a detailed report from our investigator in the coming months, which we will forward to you.
 Yours, etc
 Lord Peter Beecham
 Solicitor

***

Sowrithil, Devon, 16 December 1846

Lord Beecham,
 I require an update to my will. Details enclosed.
 Report also on the status of my query regarding an Enduring Trust to maintain the upkeep of Sowrithil. I am disappointed I have had to enquire as to an update.
 Signed
 His Grace, the Duke of Sowrith

***

Beecham & Co Chambers, London, 25 February 1847

Dear Etta,

Why are you sending me such letters? Do you mean to cause me no end of angst? You cannot pretend to be male and attend a law society function! How long do you believe this pretence will last? Within four minutes, you would get frustrated with the charade and ruin the whole thing. I swear, you send me such missives to give me heart palpations.

Before I expire on the spot, I will write of other things and pretend you have heeded my words (though, in truth, I know you haven't). Lord Beecham has me writing correspondence for the Duke of Sowrith, if you can believe it. I don't know how it is I have so risen in his esteem to merit such a lofty appointment as, most days, I am certain he wishes to terminate my employment. However, apparently he is reluctantly admiring of the way I form my capitals— Tell Me, Etta, Do You Believe Them Worthy? I don't see what is so special about them, but am grateful Lord Beecham finds something to commend.

How is my mother? She writes, but I'm certain she glosses over the worst of it. Father is still having fits, isn't he? Will you visit and report back? Mother will know what you are about, but she can't stop you. I don't believe anyone could stop you, not when you set your mind to something. In any event, if you'll report back, I'll be your friend forever. Promise. How can you refuse such an inducement?

In all seriousness, please visit with them. It worries me, being so far away and unable to verify for myself the truth of Mother's words. I know my wages help them, and Father's stipend from the University, but it's not the same as being there.

Criminy, I will set myself to weep if I continue in this vein. Let us talk of other things. Such as law society functions. You cannot attend, Etta. It's frustrating and galling, but it's the way of the world.

All my love,

Gwen

P. S. Please don't address letters to my place of employment as Gwennie Parkes. I know you find it uproariously amusing, however I am certain Lord Beecham won't see it that way.

***

Sowrithil, Devon, 1 March 1847

Miss Parkes,

I believe you sent this letter to the incorrect address.

Sowrith

***

Beecham & Co Chambers, London, 14 March 1847

Your Grace. Sir. I cannot apologise enough. My personal correspondence must have been mixed with Lord Beecham's correspondence.

Again, I apologise profusely.

Sincerely,

Miss Gwendolyn Parkes

***

Sowrithil, Devon, 20 March 1847

Miss Parkes,
Do not leave me in suspense. Did Etta attend the Law Society function dressed as a man?
Sowrith

***

Beecham & Co Chambers, London, 28 March 1847

Your Grace,
I am not certain we should correspond. I have made an egregious error in sending my personal correspondence to you and do not wish to trouble you with personal matters.
Sincerely,
Miss Gwendolyn Parkes
P.S. Etta did not attend the Law Society function dressed as a man. She attended as a serving maid instead. She is trying to kill me, I am certain.

***

Sowrithil, Devon, 3 April 1847

Miss Parkes,
Surely such a disguise could not have been productive?
Sowrith

***

Beecham & Co Chambers, London, 10 April 1847

Your Grace,
Apparently, it was. Her last letter was abuzz with the knowledge she gleaned from the function. I cannot think how she built the nerve to attend such, but then she has always been thus. When we were girls together in Cambridge, she led and I followed. Of course, she led without a backward glance or the barest notion of a plan, and I followed picking up the pieces. But, Your Grace, I cannot have you thinking I would want it any other way. Etta forced me to actions I would never have attempted on my own, and I am a better person for it.

Oh, dear. I am running on with events and discourse that cannot be of interest. Your Grace, do you require me to pass a message to Lord Beecham at all?

Miss Gwendolyn Parkes

***

Sowrithil, Devon, 26 April 1847

Miss Parkes,
No message is required.
Are your parents well?
Sowrith

***

Beecham & Co Chambers, London, 7 May 1847

Your Grace,
Yes, I thank you, sir; as well as can be expected.

Are you certain I cannot pass a message?
Miss Parkes

***

Sowrithil, Devon, 17 May 1847

Miss Parkes,
There is no message. I enjoy corresponding with you. You have a way with a turn of phrase that is...pleasing. I find I should like more of your turns of phrase. If you are amenable.
The weather here is nice.
Sowrith

***

Beecham & Co Chambers, London, 1 June 1847

Your Grace,
If you believe my turn of phrase pleasing, I am vain enough not to dissuade you.
Of course, now I cannot think of a single thing to write! Everything seems trite and forced. However, I shall persevere and attempt to write something that is vaguely amusing.
I would venture to say the weather here in London is nice as well. Of course, there is no great distance between Devon and London that would make such an observation overwhelmingly brilliant, but then I have heard the moors of Dartmoor are subject to their own whims. Is it grey? Windy? I should think it would be.
I am used to the industry of London and the greenery of Cambridge. Some days, I miss the clean

air of Cambridge, where I'd sit in my parents' garden and watch the university students bicycle to their next class. My father was a professor before his illness, and of a time former students would come to visit.

But this cannot be of interest. I am sorry, Your Grace. It is only I miss home.

Miss Parkes

***

Sowrithil, Devon, 14 June 1847

Miss Parkes,

The sky here was blue for half a moment, long enough to remind me of how an unstormy clime appears. The wind even ceased as if cowed by the appearance of weak sunlight upon the moors.

I went for a walk through the rocks and crags and found some wildlife had thought to do the same. A hound lapped at water trapped by rock, though he froze when he spied me and did not move again until I'd passed.

I understand your need for green. I travelled to London once and found I missed the roar of the wind tearing through the spires and turrets of Sowrithil and the skies, while grey, were not the same grey.

You have inspired me to creativity with my words, Miss Parkes. I hope you find them pleasing.

Sowrith

***

Beecham & Co Chambers, London, 30 June 1847

Your Grace,

Your words are beautiful. I can picture the moors as you described, and the mangy hound—was he mangy? I feel certain he must have been from your description.

You've been to London but once? It seems a man of your stature should come to Town more. Although I do not mean to question you, I was only surprised. However, I am not one to talk. I can well understand the appeal of remaining in one's home. I feel certain some days I will expire from missing mine.

Thank you for your letter. It brightened an otherwise dreary day.

Miss Parkes

***

Sowrithil, Devon, 9 July 1847

Dear Miss Parkes,

The rock of the tors collected rain today in pools of silver that reflected the clouds overhead. Touching it rippled the pristine surface, leaving a fine sheen against the dark rock in the pool's edge.

I remained seated on the tor, my hair a lash against my closed eye. I find peace in such a time, the roar of the wind a lullaby and the burn on my skin a comfort. Do you believe this makes me odd?

I should say attending London only once in my life makes me decidedly odd. It is only—I have scars, Miss Parkes. They are noticeable. When I am not at Sowrithil, they are...noticed. It is not a comfortable thing.

If you should like, you may call me Sowrith. Perhaps even, you might like—That is, I should like it if you would address me as—My given name is Edward.

The weather here is nice. It seems autumn is about to begin. The wind has been subdued.

Sowrith

***

Beecham & Co Chambers, London, 21 July 1847

Dear Edward,

Your letter was well timed. I have not been experiencing the best of times. My mother wrote my father has taken a turn. It is nothing to be concerned with, she writes, but she lies. She lies to protect me, and I won't have the truth of it until Etta responds with the reality. I do not like being so far from them without the wherewithal to visit and assure myself of their health.

However, I will content myself with the knowledge Etta will respond without delay, and I will soon have the truth of it. It will be nothing, as my mother says. It will, won't it, Edward?

As always, your letter cheered me. Your descriptions are wonderful, and I feel I am there beside you, fingers trailing in the shallow pool as the wind whips around us. It would be a fine thing indeed to see the world as you do, the beauty in even the harshest of places.

What do you think of London? What beauty could you find in this smoke-shrouded city? I find myself at a loss to discern loveliness when a longing for home consumes me.

My, but that turned morbid fast!

I am sorry, Edward. It was not my intention to

transfer my burdens to you. Instead, I shall endeavour to lift your spirits. I did see something pretty the other day, a bright swatch of cloth in a dressmaker's store. It was from the Orient, a kaleidoscope of reds and oranges, and a whole vista was written on the pattern, village life as it must have been one hundred years ago. I stared at it for the longest time, lost in the colours and the imaginings of a life so very different to mine.

Well. I suppose there is beauty, should you look for it.

I hope this finds you well, Edward. And I am,
Gwen

***

Sowrithil, Devon, 2 August 1847

Dear Gwen,
I wish I could offer you comfort. I wish I could assure you your parents will be well and your worry is needless. However, I cannot do these things. All I can do is offer my hope Etta will send her report soon, and that it will be favourable.

And, if it pleases you, I can offer descriptions of Sowrithil and its surrounds. My walk today comprised the western portion of the estate, which was especially hard on my leg, but then that is part of the reason I undertake this exercise. The greenery is sparse, trees bowing before the ferociousness of the wind buffeting the moors. This is the part of the estate that opens onto the wildness of the tors and hills, and my clothes were plastered to me as I fought the push.

This, I hope, eases you, if only a little.
Edward

***

Beecham & Co Chambers, London, 13 August 1847

Dear Edward,
Your words mean more than I can say. I can't—
All I can write is thank you. I hope one day I can give
you the comfort you have afforded me so completely.
Gwen

***

Sowrithil, Devon, 20 August 1847

Dear Gwen,
You give me comfort with each letter I receive. I
look forward to your letters, have I ever told you? I
sit in my study and I make sure all other work is
cleared from my desk before I open them. I'll read
them quickly, and then I'll read them again, slower
and able to smile at your humour and frown at your
dismay. Sometimes, I take them on the moors and I'll
climb to the top of a rock formation to read them as
the wind howls around me.
Or rather, I imagine I would do so. My leg
prevents the climb of anything higher than a foot. (I
must inform you this was intended as humour I am
told I can be thought dour.)
How is London?
Edward

***

Beecham & Co Chambers, London, 30 August 1847

Dear Edward,

I must confess, I hoard your letters upon their receipt. I torture myself with waiting until I am alone in my room, the lamp lit and the day behind me before I savour your words. Is it odd we do this, do you think? Or is it simply a sign our friendship is strong?

I am certain one day we will meet, whether it is in the smoke and fog of London or the wind-swept plains of Dartmoor. I cannot believe our friendship is one that will never spill from the page to real life. Although this is forward of me, is it not? I suppose the unsettlement I feel at the present is prompting me to rashness. Maybe it will be later I will wish these words unwritten, but I cannot regret it now.

I could write of Cambridge, of the river lined with trees and the punts on a clear summer's day, but my words won't approach yours for beauty. One day, I should like to see the moors as you do. It would be a sight to behold.

Gwen

***

Beecham & Co Chambers, London, 2 September 1847

Dear Edward,

I apologise for this letter, but I feel I must write and vent my anger or I shall explode.

There has been an Incident here at the chambers. That is how Lord Beecham refers to it, capitalized as if it foretells the end of the world.

Edward. This is what happened.

I was working on a transcript when the door to

my scribing room flew open to reveal one of Lord Beecham's most premier clients. Not yourself, of course, but another. I, as you can imagine, was startled. The room set aside for my use is far from the main thoroughfare of the chambers and I rarely receive visitors without some purpose for their presence. This man, he opened the door and, after a brief moment of speechlessness, demanded to know who I was. I, in turn, had lost all semblance of voice. How could I respond, Edward? It had been intimated for the entirety of my career at Lord Beecham's chambers that I was to remain unknown and hidden. How could I answer his query?

After what felt like forever, the head clerk arrived and ushered the client from the room. I can only imagine the discussion that took place following our encounter, for when I arrived at work this morning, I was called to Lord Beecham's side.

I have been reprimanded, Edward. I have been told I am too forward and I was at fault for the whole encounter. I have been told I am lucky to still have employment, and only the condescension and preference some clients show for my hand has saved me. I have been told, again, that I am employed only by grace of the largess Lord Beecham shows me.

God in Heaven, I am so, so angry. This is beyond all comprehension. How could I be held at fault for an encounter that occurred purely by chance? How could I be the one to bear this wrong, to be the one who must be circumspect, to be hidden and shunned and then because of one client's loss of direction, I am to bring the chambers to its knees? How could I—

I am sorry, Edward. My frustration escapes me. It is the same tune, over and again. I am to be held to *a different standard, because I am female. Perhaps Etta has the right of it. Maybe it is we should invade law functions dressed as maids. It seems if we attempt legitimate employment, we are punished for it.*

My apologies again for this letter, Edward. It is only I feel better once I've set my thoughts on paper, and it brings me comfort to know you read them.

Gwen

***

Beecham & Co Chambers, London, 3 September 1847

Your Grace,

Please disregard my latest missive. It was poorly done of me. I would understand if you should not wish to correspond with me again.

Miss Parkes

***

Sowrithil, Devon, 12 September 1847

Beecham,

You are to attend me at Sowrithil. Bring a scribe with you.

Miss Parkes will suffice.

Sowrith

Chapter One

Sowrithil
Devon, England, 29 September 1847

TAPPING HER FOOT TO a manic beat, Gwen waited.

Shadows stretched across the stone floor, casting long, spindly fingers broken only by table and carpet. The weak flicker of the lamp a servant had lit a half hour before gave a movement to the shadow, making the fingers flex and retreat as if steepled by an unknown hand. The light threw a garish relief across the visage of a gargoyle, maw frozen in a sneer filled with wicked-sharp teeth. A gargoyle that, for some reason unknown, resided inside the Duke of Sowrith's principal estate, in the hall connecting the secretary's room and the duke's own study.

At the thought of the duke, her foot stuttered to a stop.

For an hour or more, she'd been seated in an uncomfortable chair in this hall, steadily becoming more chilled as the light faded. The whole of the day had been spent in travel from London to Devon to the duke's estate of Sowrithil, and she'd yet to eat or find rest of any description. Sitting in this chair could hardly be termed rest, as she'd been on edge ever since Lord Beecham had ordered her to sit while he conversed with the duke.

Gwen started tapping her foot once more. The duke. How was she to endure this wait before she met the duke?

She bit her lip. No, tell it true. Before she met *Edward*.

Hands bundled in her lap, she quieted her troublesome appendage, tucking her ankle behind its mate for good measure as a shiver rushed through her. It was an assignment like any other. *He* was an assignment like any other. She'd written him numerous times under the direction of the solicitors of the chambers, copied legal documents concerning his estate and his business matters. She'd undertaken a hundred tasks for his account, just as she had for dozens of other clients of Lord Beecham's chambers. She should not make more of this than what it was.

But then...she'd never before travelled to a client's residence. She'd never left her small, solitary room at the chambers. She'd never been directed upon her arrival for a day of work to pack a bag and meet Lord Beecham at the train station, had never travelled to Sowrithil, had never walked Sowrithil's drive, felt the crunch of gravel beneath her feet, been greeted by Edward's butler, walked Edward's halls....

She'd never before met Edward

Crossing her arms over her stomach, she leant forward, pressing deep. Good heavens, she was nervous, and excited, and *nervous*. She was going to meet *Edward*. One moment soon, he was going to open that door, and she would see him. She would see the man she'd corresponded with for over a year, to whom she'd expressed every thought, and who had expressed his to her. It did not matter that he was a duke, so far above her in consequence as to be laughable. He was her friend, and, at last, they would meet.

Foot tapping wildly, she leant her head back against the wall. This was all so ridiculous. *She* was ridiculous to have this unbridled excitement rioting through her. Exhaling, she caught the stare of the gargoyle. The gargoyle knew how ridiculous her thoughts. Its stone features laughed at her, and in a fit of pique, she poked her tongue out.

The study door opened. Leaping to her feet, she swayed as the blood rushed from her head.

Lord Beecham appeared in the door way and, his eyes lighting upon her, crooked a finger. "Miss Parkes. Come."

Heart beating a rapid tattoo, she bent to grip the handle of her carpet bag. Lord Beecham had abandoned the door by the time she had gathered herself enough to approach, the worn wooden handle of the bag pressing deep into her palm.

Passing through the door, Gwen stopped, her jaw slack as she looked about the chamber. Lit only by the flame of the massive fireplace dominating one wall and the wan flicker of a lamp seated on the enormous desk, the room was huge, cavernous even, and dark. So dark. The faint light picked up rows upon rows of books while heavy drapes of an unidentifiable fabric covered what she could only presume were windows. The floor was the same stone as the hall, the only carpet appearing before the fire under the clawed feet of a large armchair.

Her gaze returned to the fireplace. A man stood before it, his back to her, right hand held by his left.

Her heart, already racing, started a wild thud against her ribs. That was him. The duke. *Edward.*

He did not turn, though she willed him to. Willed him to turn so she could utter that most important of phrases, the one she'd longed to say for an age now.

Hello, Edward.

"Miss Parkes." Lord Beecham stood before the duke's desk, wearing a look that spoke of his impatience. He gestured at a chair set before the desk. "Sit."

Clutching her bag to her, she did as she was bidden and fought the urge to look to the fire. To Edward.

Back ramrod straight, Lord Beecham pinned her with his gaze. "Miss Parkes, the Duke of Sowrith requires your expertise in scribing his correspondence for the foreseeable future. I will be returning to London in the morning, but you will remain here at Sowrithil to undertake any direction he specifies."

Gwen blinked. She—*What?*

"Your presence here has been requested by His Grace himself. If it were my choice, I would have recommended someone with greater skill and experience. However, I cede to His Grace in this matter as will you."

She was to… *What?*

"If anyone requires contact, you are to give me their notification. I will see it delivered."

Finally, she found her voice. "Lord Beecham, I cannot—"

"Miss Parkes, do not test my patience. You are

already employed under extraordinary circumstances, and it would not take much for me to rescind those circumstances. You will do as told."

Shock began to wane. She glanced toward the fireplace, but the man standing before it didn't so much as twitch. "Sir, I cannot depart London for an undetermined period of time. I have commitments—"

Impatience darkened Lord Beecham's expression. "Of which you will tell me, and I will deal with them. Your presence is required, Miss Parkes. It is as simple as that."

Annoyance stirred, though she fought to keep it hidden. "This is extremely irregular, sir. Surely this is beyond the bounds of propriety—"

"Miss Parkes, do not presume to know my mind. The usual proprieties may be waived in this instance, but know if you step a foot out of line—"

"Beecham. Leave us."

Both she and Lord Beecham whipped their heads around. The duke stood before the fire, still with his back to them, though the hands at his back seemed held a fraction tighter.

Lord Beecham recovered his voice first. "Your Grace?"

The hands at the duke's back tightened further. "Leave."

Looking as if he bit back sour words, Lord Beecham obeyed, sketching a bow though the duke continued to regard the fire. Then he departed, leaving her alone with the duke.

Moments passed as the crackle and hiss of the fire echoed through the room, overwhelmingly loud. With no other recourse, Gwen studied the duke's back. The perfectly combed black hair long enough to rest on his collar. The width of his shoulders in his beautifully tailored jacket. The fall of his trousers. His head dipped, and it seemed to her he made as if to brace himself, his shoulders infinitesimally tensing. Then he turned.

She managed to swallow her gasp. Just.

She'd known he was scarred. He'd told her, in the briefest way possible, and she'd known, she'd *known* the brevity disguised the extent of his injury. But even knowing those scant words hid much could not have prepared her for the reality.

Light threw itself across his face and form to fall upon the thick white scar that snaked across his face, starting somewhere in the thickness of his dark brown hair. The scar bisected his forehead before disappearing under the patch that covered his left eye only to begin again to cut deep into his cheek. Twisting toward the corner of his mouth, the scar drew his lip into a perpetual sneer before ending beneath his chin.

She bit her cheek to keep from offering words she knew he did not wish. Lord above. So much pain.

Turning his cheek to display his right side, he made his way to his desk, a slight limp to his left leg marring his step. Lowering himself to the seat, he placed his right hand on the polished surface of the desk and his left on the leather blotter. Then he raised his gaze to her.

He said nothing, his face impassive, bar that involuntary sneer. His eye was as unrevealing as the eye-patch—a dark, dark brown that gave nothing away. The hand that lay on the leather blotter was twisted and broken, the two smallest fingers frozen while a network of fine white scars ran across the back of his hand to disappear into his coat sleeve.

"Did you have a pleasant journey?"

His right hand held for her a strange fascination. Did he write his letters with that hand? "Your Grace?"

The hand on the blotter twitched. "Your journey. Was it pleasant?"

Forcing herself to drag her gaze from his hand, she instead regarded a region near his chin as was proper for someone so much greater in consequence than her. "Yes."

Silence again. How could she have such silence with Edward? How was it they were not conversing, as they did in their letters, with the ease granted to the closest of friends? How was it she was trapped here with this silent duke, who regarded her so dispassionately and destroyed every foolish hope she'd entertained?

"Your time here won't be purely work."

"Your Grace?" Lord, she sounded the fool, repeating his title, but how else was she to respond when he abruptly delivered a statement as if she should know his thoughts?

"You may take a half day on Saturdays and a full day on Sundays. Any other time when you are not scribing, you may employ as you see fit under the proviso you are easily contactable should you be required. Is this agreeable?"

No. Criminy, *no*. None of this was agreeable. Or sensible. Or…or… She could not make head nor tail of any of this.

"Miss Parkes?"

Bewildered, she saw no other recourse but to agree. She nodded.

It seemed to her the tension with which he held himself relaxed. Slightly. "Excellent. You will tell Dobson what is required for a long term stay. He will arrange to have anything you require brought from your lodgings."

How long was she expected to remain? She couldn't stay indefinitely. She had commitments in London, not to mention a need to collect her wages each week. She had no arrangement in place to send a portion of her earnings to her parents, and she would *not* speak of such things to Lord Beecham.

Silence again. Her tongue seemed tied, and she could not unravel it for the life of her. She wanted to speak of their letters, to ask if he were their author, but that steady, dispassionate stare forbade such a familiar question. It could not be him. He could not have written those letters. Surely he would say something? Surely, if he had, their acquaintance would not have started with a decree and a complete disregard of her opinion. And he hadn't answered her last letter, hadn't said whether he wished their correspondence to continue. Oh Lord, he hadn't *said*.

The smallest twitch to his expression, and she wondered if he wanted to say something. Would he speak now of their correspondence? Would he smile and become Edward?

He said nothing.

Disappointment burned through her. She ducked her head, and hoped he wouldn't notice the sheen to her eyes.

"You should rest. A tray will be brought to your room." He straightened his back, his posture rigid. "You may go."

She nodded again. Clutching her bag, she started toward the door. Finally remembering the manners her mother had taught her, she turned and curtsied. "Good night, Your Grace."

Something again flickered in his dark, dark eye. "Good night, Miss Parkes."

Chapter Two

THE WIND SCREAMED ALONG the unseen windows. Gloom shrouded the chamber in a heavy presence that crept over the furnishings and slid down the walls. The bed hangings offered a protection of sorts, a barrier between the unknown terrors of the dark and safe haven.

Gwen stared at the canopy above her bed, doing her level best to ignore each shriek of the wind. Even after the day of travel, after sitting unoccupied for hours, even though she was so tired her eyes felt like they were full of sand, she couldn't sleep.

It wasn't only the wind, though. The chamber she'd been given unnerved her. It was by far the largest and grandest room she'd ever slept in, the bed so big she could stretch out both arms and not touch the sides. She'd spent a good hour examining every inch of the chamber, opening every cupboard, investigating the room reserved solely for clothes. Lord above, a wardrobe you could walk into. In London, her clothes were kept covered by a sheet on a rail in one corner of her lodgings. Truth be told, her entire *lodgings* would probably fit in the wardrobe room.

It also unnerved her she'd somehow become an unwilling guest at Sowrithil.

Outrage, a steady rise since this afternoon, erupted and she hit at the sheets. What was she *doing* here? She should be back in London, in her own bed, ignoring the sounds of the street below, not jumping every time the Dartmoor wind screamed past. There was no indication of how long she would remain here or even what her duties were to be. Oh no, she was supposed to be a good little girl and do as she was told. *We're upending your life, Miss Parkes. Be damned to propriety and only be grateful, for we can take it from you with a word.*

She could not even fathom why the duke had brought her here. She'd thought... Well, her thoughts had turned out to be incorrect, hadn't they? The man she'd known as Edward probably didn't even exist. Probably, for some reason known only to him, the duke had decided to toy with her, to create the fiction of a friendship between them, and he'd brought her here for some jape she'd yet to discover.

Or…maybe it hadn't even been him who wrote her. Maybe it was someone on his staff, signing his name and making her think...making her believe...

Wrenching herself upright, she rubbed her eyes with her hand and ignored the wetness she found there. Focusing on outrage, she rubbed her temples. It was so unfair. She could not protest, for Lord Beecham would snatch her employment from her without a moment's hesitation and she needed her position. Her parents relied upon the income she sent them. She was beyond fortunate to obtain this employment, which was both well-paying and in the industry she loved. She had not thought to be able to work in law; had thought the limitations of her gender would again keep her from something she loved. However, somehow she'd stumbled into this work and she would not lose it over this.

Maybe it was she couldn't protest her presence here, but she would damn well do something about her sleeplessness. Damned if she was going to toss and turn like a fool when there was a whole study full of books downstairs. She didn't care if it was the duke's private domain. She didn't care if she was trespassing. She would go there, find a book, maybe even read it in his hallowed room. Besides, he'd be abed by now, and it was the one room in this whole creaking monolith she knew.

Throwing back the covers, Gwen shoved out of bed. Grabbing the lamp set on the dresser, she stormed from the room.

As she stalked through the halls, thoughts whirled about her head. How dare he write her those letters, those beautiful, meaningful letters, and then act as if they did not know each other? As if they were nothing? He'd looked right through her, discounted her wishes or opinion, and treated her as if...as if she were a servant. Well, if he wanted to act that way, who was she to argue? She was happy to pretend they'd never corresponded, that she'd never shared her fears with him, that he'd never told her of his scars. She was *glad* to not have to converse at such depth with him.

Wiping at her cheeks, she looked around her. Somehow, she'd remembered the way to the study, and now she stood before the huge oak doors. The door bowed to her will, swinging open obediently and allowing her entry.

A fire burned low in the fireplace, casting

strange and terrible patterns on the walls. Unease skittered along her spine, bringing with it a chill. Setting her jaw, she lifted the lamp higher. She refused to by cowed by the dark. The bookcase beckoned, and she went to it, examining only the books illuminated by the light, not the shadows that lurked behind.

Her eyebrows rose as she read the titles before her. Rows upon rows upon rows of Gothic novels. From what surely must be every novel Mrs. Radcliffe ever published to titles by Lewis and Walpole. Mary Shelly's mad scientist novel was represented as well as a whole raft by someone named Poe. She frowned. Those volumes looked newer than the rest, the spines barely cracked, while those by Mrs. Radcliffe had the look of having been read hundreds of times.

She picked one, sliding it from the shelf to turn it over in her hand. She'd not heard of it, but then the publisher's mark read only last year. If nothing else, she would have fear as the reason for being awake rather than anger.

A loud, sudden bang rang through the study.

Dropping the book from a suddenly nerveless hand, she, through some miracle, kept hold of the lamp. Heart racing, she whipped around. The light threw the shadows into chaos, but nothing leapt out at her, no beastie set upon devouring her whole.

Telling herself to calm, she knelt to pick up the book. It had most likely been the wind beating at a shutter somewhere. Forcing her breath to an even keel, she turned her attention back to the book in her hands. A reluctant smile took her as she read the overwrought text of the first page. If nothing else, this would take her mind from her troubles with its sheer ridiculousness.

Closing the book with a snap, she raised the lamp to look at the other titles.

Another noise, this one closer, quieter.

Her heart pounding, she stared at the titles before her. It would be nothing again, though it didn't sound like a shutter. No, it sounded like a footstep, one muffled to disguise its tread.

She shook herself. *Gwendolyn Parkes, stop being a ninny.* It was nothing, and she would not entertain the notion it was more than that by looking... Oh criminy, she had to look.

Breath caught in chest, she whirled around. See, how foolish was she, there was nothing—

She almost dropped the book again.

The Duke of Sowrith stood, ramrod straight, before the fire.

Dumbly, she stared at him. It was all well and good when defiance was theoretical, but now that he stood before her in an advanced state of dishabille and with his face in shadow... Well, if she were wearing boots, she would be shaking in them.

Lifting her chin, she pretended bravery. "Your Grace."

A long silence, in which he moved not at all, merely stood before the fire, shrouded in shadow and flame. Then, "Miss Parkes. Good evening."

Setting her jaw, she lifted her chin a little higher. Lord, this place drove her to fancy. Shadow and flame indeed. Next, she would be running across the moors in her nightgown, hair a dull brown streak behind her. But then, only raven-haired beauties were foolish enough to run barefoot through uneven ground, or at least, such was purported by those who wrote the literature in her hand.

Silence stretched between them, filled with the

faint crackle of the dying fire.

"May I help you with something?" the duke finally asked.

"I—No." Wetting her lips, she held up the book, keeping her gaze fixed somewhere over his right shoulder. "I couldn't sleep."

"Ah."

Again, silence. The book felt heavy in her hand, her fingers aching from clutching it too tight.

"Why can you not sleep?"

Incredulity forced her gaze. His face was still hidden in shadow, but surely he could not seriously be asking why—

Fury roared unchecked through her. "Why can I not sleep? Well, let me think." Fingers trembling with rage, she tapped her temple. "Could it be the wind screaming past this mausoleum of a house, loud enough to wake the dead? Or is it the room I've been given is three times the size of my lodgings in London, enough that I got lost on the way to the bed? Perhaps it is because I've been travelling all day and though that has exhausted me, apparently I am not exhausted enough to sleep." Chest tight, her mouth stretched into a garish smile. "Or maybe it's because I've been *ordered* to remain here, in direct contradiction to my wishes and with no means of refusal."

"You were not told you might be staying here longer."

It should have been a question. It irritated her enormously that he had framed it as a statement. Her fingers dug into the book. "Clearly, I was not. The first I heard of it was in Lord Beecham's presence and yours."

The duke stepped forward, his left leg dragging

slightly. Light fell across his features, revealing an expression that still showed little. She drew in her breath as light also fell upon the cruel twist of his scars, and she hated herself a little when his lips tightened at her gasp. "I apologise, Miss Parkes. It was not my intention to bring you discomfort."

He might not have intended it, but that was exactly what had occurred.

"If it is so disagreeable to you, you may leave with the next stage to the train station," he said stiffly.

Oh yes. That was a completely viable solution.

She blinked. Wait a minute. Were they talking of the same thing? Surely he did not think his scars...

He took another step forward, then seemed unsure if he should continue. A strange expression drawing his features, he hovered there, halfway between one step and the next. He settled at the end of the bookcase, his pose rather awkward. "You came for a book?"

"Yes." He was behaving...oddly. Not at all like the standoffish man he'd been but moments before. "There seems rather a lot of Gothic literature."

"Oh. Well, yes, I..." It was only then he seemed to realise his dishabille and a redness that could only be a blush stained his cheeks. Rolling down his sleeves, he said, "Gothic literature interests me."

Gothic literature? Truly?

"The collection is the finest that could be amassed and encompasses all the eras," he continued. "You will find tales from the Americas, as well as the German classics. Do you speak German?"

It seemed to her he looked expectant as if he wished to know her every thought on the Gothics, and for him to impart his along with his enthusiasm for the subject. It was too much, too fast. How could he go from disdain and distance to this almost desperate grasp at commonality? Would that he'd had such expectation when Lord Beecham was ordering her to stay. Throat working, she closed her eyes. That thought was unkind and beneath her dignity.

"Miss Parkes?"

His voice sounded…uncertain. Rousing herself, she recalled his question. "No, Your Grace. It is not something my mother thought to teach me. I would venture to say this is because *she* does not speak German." She must have imagined his uncertainty. His expression held no trace of the emotion.

He cocked his head. "Your mother was a governess before her marriage, was she not? I thought perhaps the Germanic languages would have been part of her curriculum."

Mouth agape, she stared at him. He *was* the one who had written those letters. He had written her, and now she was here in his study with him, she in her nightgown and he in his shirtsleeves and—

The inappropriateness of this whole situation crashed over her. Oh, criminy. She couldn't do this. She could talk of defiance, but she was not made as Etta was. She could not do it. The need to escape wound inside her, desperate and undeniable. "I will disturb you no longer. I have my book, and I will leave you to your contemplation."

"Stay, Miss Parkes. I... That is, you might find the later period of interest." He took half a step toward her.

Clutching the book to her, she backed away from him. "I have to go, Your Grace."

Like a shutter drawn, his expression turned to indifference. Ramrod straight, he laced his hands behind his back. "Of course, Miss Parkes. My apologies for keeping you. Good night."

With a tight smile, she curtsied and left before he could say anything further.

Chapter Three

STARING AT THE HEAVY curtains, Gwen laced her fingers in her lap and waited.

For over two hours, she'd been seated alone in the duke's study with no direction or clue as to what was supposed to happen. She'd arrived at nine of the clock, inkwell, pen and notebook in hand. Now, it had just gone a quarter after eleven, the chime of the clock on the duke's mantle fading into the ether, and he'd still not arrived.

Needless to say, she was somewhat irritated.

After their ill-advised meeting last night, she'd made it back to her room without incident and then had spent most of the night staring at the canopy above her bed. She'd not even managed a chapter or two of the book she'd appropriated, the tome abandoned to the bedside table. Instead, she'd run over and again in her mind what he'd said...or what little he'd said, and on Gothic novels, of all things. He could not put two words together about important things like asking if someone would be amenable to contract work for an indeterminate amount of time, but he could wax lyrical on Mr. Poe and Mrs.

Radcliffe and the Germanic Gothics. Germanic, for heaven's sake.

Lord, she was sick of sitting here. Launching to her feet, she shoved her pens and papers onto the duke's desk and strode over to the curtains. They'd been driving her insane since she'd arrived, the heavy fabric blocking what little sun this part of the world had. She wrenched them open, the curtains dragging a protest as a fine sprinkle of dust rained upon her. Weak sunlight filtered through, hurting her eyes but a moment before she adjusted to the faint glare. Framed by the panes, the gardens led down to the moors where a darkening sky loomed over distant crags of rock.

Crossing her arms, Gwen curled her hands over her biceps. The vista was not unexpected. It seemed all of Sowrithil was the same, a brief ring of tamed green falling away to a landscape full of dramatic juts of rock reaching toward a threatening grey sky. It seemed not to matter what time of day it was, either. This morning, she'd raced to the drive to catch Lord Beecham before he'd departed and been confronted with the same.

She stared out the window. She'd wanted to talk with Lord Beecham, to plead her case for returning to London. However, her pleas had only fallen upon deaf ears. In point of fact, he'd elaborated upon her expected duties, ordering her to undertake whatever the duke commanded. *Whatever* he commanded of her.

Hands tightening on her biceps, she glared at the moors as impotent anger and disbelief coursed through her once more. Lord Beecham had intimated that if the duke wished to greater intimacies with her person, she was not to refuse. It was completely beyond the realms of comprehension that Lord Beecham thought it appropriate to say such to her. Besides the fact it was a truly deplorable thing to intimate, it was in direct contradiction to her employer's almost daily edict that she prescribe to behaviour of a ridiculously strict nature.

What happened to his insistence his law firm would be ruined should it be discovered he employed that most dreaded of things, a *female*, as a scribe, and one so brash as to insist on employment? While others in his employ were able to do as they wished, she was required to stay in the background, quiet as a mouse. She was even required to dress in browns and greys, keep her hair scraped into a bun, and her gaze was never to meet any clients, should she be so inopportune as to meet one. All of this, and yet she was to allow the duke her body should he ask?

Her fingers dug into her flesh. She was so sick of this. She was sick of wearing brown. She was sick of being ignored. She was sick of being treated as if she were less than nothing, as if her wishes and thoughts were meaningless.

And she was sick of waiting.

Turning on her heel, she abandoned her quills, her papers. If he could not be bothered to direct her, than she would not be bothered waiting.

She left the room without a backwards glance.

***

ACROSS THE DESOLATE LANDSCAPE, the wind screamed, broken only by jagged rock jutting to reach toward the grey sky. Harsh green shrubbery covered the earth, the thick, gnarled branches grasping at flesh and bone as a body fought through the thicket.

Gwen ignored the sting, the wind tearing at her hair and warring with her hairpins even as it plastered her dress to her body and slowed every step. In London, there was no wind, and a film of soot and grease lingered on her skin no matter how often she washed. Here, her lips were dry, her skin parched, and she was completely and utterly exhilarated.

Unable to help herself, she grinned. Oh, it was even better than he'd described. Untamed and wild, the moors stretched on forever, full of mystery and an ominous oppression that sent an excited shiver down her spine. The earth almost hummed while the shriek of the wind created a cacophony she could never have imagined.

She wished she had the words to describe the majesty of the place. The awe-inspiring rocks jutting to the sky. The dark-streaked sky. The grey-green foliage. The feeling it engendered, deep in her breast. It made her feel wild, and exhilarated, and...free.

"Miss Parkes!"

The unexpected shout made Gwen whip around. The duke bore down on her, white-faced and furious as he limped toward her. He leant heavily on his cane, the speed of his approach seemingly aggravating his affliction.

"What do you think you're doing?" he demanded.

Blood drained from her face. Criminy, she shouldn't have left. She shouldn't have abandoned her duties so wholly, shouldn't have been so enthralled by the moors she'd forgotten her obligations. Oh Lord, her parents. She'd forgotten her parents. How they relied upon her. How her mother wouldn't admit the money Gwen sent them eased her burden. That if that money was suddenly gone, they'd suffer.

Frozen, she could only watch as the duke grew ever closer. He halted before her, his chest heaving as he took her arm in a bruising grip. "This is beyond foolishness. You cannot wander on the moors alone. You will return to Sowrithil at once."

Sudden, intense rage ignited within her. She wrenched her arm from his grasp as fury immolated any fear. "I will *not*."

His expression turned thunderous. "You will heed me in this."

A wild recklessness took hold of her. "Why?"

Perverse satisfaction ripped through her at his astonishment. "It is too dangerous—" he started.

"If I choose to break my head, it's no concern of yours." Squaring her shoulders, she dared him to comment.

He appeared completely at a loss for words. "You are my guest."

"How am I your *guest*? I've been ordered here against my will. You didn't even have the decency to attend your study this morning. What am I to think except that I am left to my own devices?"

He looked completely at a loss, but she didn't care how *he* felt. As if a seal had broken, emotion barrelled through her, a twine of rage and frustration and…and hurt. "I've chosen to wander these moors, and if I'm pursued by a dark man with murderous intent, or if I should break a leg, or if an enormous hound devours me whole, you may rest assured *you* have no say in it. In fact, I think I shall do these things just to be difficult. I rather fancy a broken leg. Perhaps if I'm incapacitated, people will stop thinking they can *order me about*."

The wind ripped between them, taking her

words with it. For the longest time he looked at her, his features slowly bleeding of all expression. "My apologies, Miss Parkes."

Her jaw dropped. *An apology? Really?*

"The danger is such that I did not curb my tongue as I should." Appearing decidedly uncomfortable, he cleared his throat. "Again, I apologise"

Oh. Well, that was…Oh. "Yes. Thank you. Your Grace."

Clearly still ill at ease, he inclined his head.

She studied his profile, carefully turned so she couldn't see the scars. Only the black band of his eye patch crossing his forehead hinted something was not quite right. He did seem as if he'd rushed, his hair askew and his boots muddy, while the line of his jaw was clenched and the knuckles clutching his cane were white… Was he in pain?

Guilt stirred within her. She'd never meant to cause him pain and now that rage had run its course, she must have sounded the veriest harridan. "Perhaps it wouldn't be so dangerous if someone guided me."

Clearing his throat, he turned his contemplation toward the tor in the distance.

Disappointment flooded her. Was he never going to talk of their letters?

"You slept well?"

His question broke her thoughts. "I beg your pardon, Your Grace?"

"After you left the library. Did you sleep well?" With his attention still on that distant tor, it was almost as if he'd not spoken at all.

"Oh. Yes. I did." Well, she had slept well, once she had finally fallen asleep. "And you? How did you sleep? Your Grace," she hastened to add.

"I slept tolerably." He lapsed into silence once more.

Oh, Lord, could this get any worse? It was he who had written the letters, she was almost certain of it. Why else react with embarrassment when she alluded to their correspondence? Why else bring her here to his estate in the middle of Devon on what could only be a pretext? Later, perhaps, she would admonish him over interfering so wholly in her life, but for now...for now, she wanted to converse with her friend.

Though every part of her screamed apprehension and uncertainty, she lifted her hand toward him and, oh-so-lightly, placed her fingers upon his forearm. "Could you... That is, will you describe them to me? The moors, I mean?"

He did not soften, remaining as unyielding as the rocks before them. "They are there before you, Miss Parkes."

"I know, but..." *In for a penny...* "You described them so beautifully in your letters."

His head whipped around, and his single eye held an astonishment he quickly shuttered. She swallowed, but she would not look away.

"My letters?" he asked carefully.

She nodded. "I used to love your descriptions. I'd read them over and again, and they'd make me feel as if I were actually there." She laughed, and even to her, it sounded a little desperate. "Or, I suppose, here."

The wind rushed to fill the silence that fell between them.

"I enjoyed writing those descriptions," he said softly.

Elation came over her, and relief, and

apprehension, and a strange kind of fear. It *was* he who had written her.

"I often think the rocks look like alters." His gaze locked on the formation before them.

She couldn't tear hers from him. "How so?"

"A few have tops flattened by the vagaries of nature. I can imagine a priestess of a thousand years gone kneeling atop them, face turned to the harsh clime as the wind whips her hair about her. Her hands would plunge into the trickle of water gathered in the crevices, and she would beseech her gods for a break in the weather, for the sun to appear after an age away." Leaning heavily on his cane, he turned to her. "Can you not see it?"

She could, now that he'd described it. The rock before them became a place of worship, a monument to religion and belief.

"Do you think they really did worship upon it?" she asked, her voice a hush.

Cocking his head, he said, "I've no idea."

For the longest time, they stared. Terribly aware of how close he stood beside her, Gwen linked her fingers and tried not to think on how little effort it would require to lay her hand over his. "Do you think we should investigate?"

He opened his mouth as if to speak, but then the strangest expression came over his face. Like a shutter, his features closed. "We should return to the house."

Disappointment crashed over her. What had changed that he would remove himself from her so?

"Come, Miss Parkes. The day is wasting, and there is work to be done." He held out his right hand.

Throat working, she stared at his offered appendage. He wore no glove, his palm smooth and unblemished. His coat and shirtsleeves rode up a little, displaying the vulnerable skin of his wrist with its faint tracery of blue veins.

She hadn't worn gloves either. Hesitantly, she slid her hand in his.

Warm and strong, his fingers closed about hers. Her breath stuttered in her chest, and she could not remove her gaze from their joined hands. It seemed to her even the wind had ceased, the whole of the world focused on her hand in his.

Then he took her hand and placed it on his left forearm. Loss filled her even as she told herself it was ridiculous to feel such.

"Miss Parkes—" His voice cracked. Red collared his ears as he cleared his throat. "Let us walk."

Nodding, she allowed him to lead her over the terrain, his footing sure even as he leant on his cane. They spoke not at all, and when they returned to Sowrithil, he led her to the study and began a dictation almost as if they'd never been on the moors.

Then he kept her too busy to think of anything but the paper before her.

Chapter Four

ABSENTLY MASSAGING HIS LEFT, Edward stared into the fire. The flames licked at the tumble of logs, turning the wood to glow scarlet. Intense heat battered against his face, pushed deep into his muscles and bones, giving some relief from the dull throb running the left side of his body.

Pain bolted through him as he hit a particularly gnarled knot of muscle. Grimly, he dug his thumb into the knot, ignoring the protest his ruined flesh made. The pain spoke of the muscle's overuse that day, of picking across the moors and undulating ground, but he counted the price his body demanded worth the time he'd spent with Miss Parkes.

With Gwen.

Closing his eye, he savoured her name as he pictured her. Gwen. She was more than he could have imagined, a mix of caution and boldness he found endlessly alluring. Her wide grey eyes, clear and direct, had studied him unwaveringly while the wisps of light-brown hair the wind had torn from the too-tight bun low on her neck haloed her face. A faint sprinkle of freckles dotted her straight nose, a particularly dark one flirting with the corner of her mouth.

He wanted to taste that freckle.

Leaning his head back, he swore softly. As if she would allow such a thing. He had handled everything badly from the moment she'd arrived at Sowrithil. He'd wanted to impress her, to have her smile and greet him warmly, and for them to find the easy conversation they'd found in their letters.

Against his misgivings— Bloody hell. Throat working, he shook his head. *Speak it true, man.* Against his downright *terror*, he'd concocted a plan to bring her to Sowrithil. In his head, it had been a brilliant idea. In his head, he'd been verbose and suave, able to speak to her with something approaching normalcy. But that had been in his head.

In reality, he'd become tongue-tied as soon as she'd entered the room. In reality, he had stood like a great lunk as her employer had mocked and insulted her, only to finally inform her she was to remain at Sowrithil. Edward had seen her shock and her dismay. He'd seen her quick glance at him as if she sought his denial or, at the least, a word of comfort. He hadn't even offered her that.

Viciously, he dug his fingers into his thigh. Bloody hell, what a grand plan he'd had. Bring her to Sowrithil, only to destroy whatever friendship they boasted. *Well done, man.*

This morning had been a disaster. He'd dressed and then stared at himself in the mirror, trying to force the first step to the study. He'd stared at the ugly twist of scars down the left side of his face, the blankness of the patch disguising the ruin of his eye. How could he present himself to her, when he was so wholly broken?

So he'd remained in his chambers, telling himself he did her a favour. Telling himself she did not wish his company, and should not be forced to such out of politeness. Telling himself this, though he only half-believed it.

He scowled at the fireplace. Damn it, he was a duke. A bloody peer of the realm. He should not be cowering in his room because he could not think of how to speak to a woman.

But it was Gwen. He didn't want to bugger it all up.

Stretching out his leg, he buried his head in his hand. Then he'd discovered she'd ventured upon the moors, and any fear or misgivings had disappeared in the face of terror. He'd torn from the house and spent a wretched half hour searching for her, certain she was broken in a ditch somewhere, her glorious grey eyes closed forever. She'd been on the moors without escort and without awareness of the dangers she faced when he'd spent his life walking the moors, using them to build strength in his ruined leg, learning their beauty…and their dangers. His relief upon finding her had been consuming, so much so that he'd completely destroyed whatever good will remained.

Forcing himself straight once more, he dug his fingers again into his thigh and wrestled with the protesting muscle. He should have stuck to the letters. He was better amongst the rocks and the wind, and writing of both. He was better on paper. In person, things fell apart.

"Good evening, Your Grace."

His heart seized in his chest. *Gwen.* He leapt to his feet, his leg protesting such a sudden move. Wincing, he offered a stunted bow, awkward and bent. "Miss Parkes. Good evening."

Standing just inside the study door, she offered a hesitant smile. "May I join you?"

Heat rose on his neck, and his ears burned. Bloody hell, she was so pretty. "Of course." Should he drag another chair to the fire? He only had one, and she would surely wish to sit.

"I hope I am not disturbing you, Your Grace. I could not sleep and thought to..." She held up a book.

The book she'd borrowed the other night. "You wish another?"

A frown creased her brow. "I'm not sure. I cannot decide if I enjoyed it."

Hoping she didn't notice, he wiped his hands on his trousers. "What makes you say that?"

"I don't know." Her brows drew further. "They are rather...atmospheric, aren't they?"

"I believe that is the point."

She made a face. "Very funny, Edward. I know that's the point. I'm just unsure if I have the right temperament to enjoy the point. I find them a bit grim for my liking."

His breath strangled in his chest. She had called Edward.

Blithely unaware, she continued, "Do you truly like them?"

Unable to speak, he nodded.

"What is it you like about them?"

Finally, he recovered his voice. "I don't know. I just do."

She wrinkled her nose. "That's no reason, Your Grace. You must have a reason for liking them."

Back to his title. He shouldn't feel such disappointment that she didn't use his given name. "I think..." What *did* he like about them? "I think it's the terror."

Her brows lifted. "Oh?"

"Yes." He allowed memories and impressions of the novels to wash over him. "The way they can shorten your breath and make you jump when you read them under cover of darkness, bed hangings drawn. You hear a creak on the stairs. A chill creeps up your spine, and you're certain someone…or something…is striding toward your room. The floorboards creak, and then the hall groans, and you are certain—you are absolutely certain—something comes for you. Something grim. Dark. Terrifying. You clutch your bed clothes to your chin, and you wait, breath strangled in your chest, for that *something* to approach, for it to grow close enough for you to spy its outline in the darkness, even as you dread the very same. You light a candle and the dark is banished, and you realise it was all in your head. However…the exhilaration remains, and you know you want to experience it again." Tips of his ears burning, his voice died away. Somehow, he'd lost himself in words.

Hand tucked under her chin, Gwen regarded him with something akin to fascination. "I should never have thought such a thing of Gothic novels."

"No?" Now the rest of him was uncomfortably hot as if his burning ears saw fit to consume him whole.

"You have such a way of describing things. You know, I should never have wanted to visit the moors if not for your descriptions."

Of course his head immediately emptied of anything intelligent to say.

"Truly." Removing her hand from under her chin, she placed it on his forearm.

He looked down. Gloveless, her fingers were

stained with ink, and they looked small and capable against the sleeve of his jacket. Raising his gaze, grey eyes captured his solitary one, such that he could not tear himself away.

It could have been a moment or it could have been a hundred before she broke their gaze, a faint flush staining her cheeks. "How was your evening, Your Grace?"

Bloody hell, his head was still empty. "I had paperwork," he finally managed.

"You must have been busy. You weren't at dinner."

"Yes. I was. Busy" Pulse a thunder in his head, he wiped his hands on his trousers. Again.

Smile dimming, she studied him. "Dinner was an interesting experience. I thought my bedchamber was cavernous, but the dining room puts it to shame."

"Yes." Again he lapsed into silence. What was wrong with him? Why could he not string two words together to form a complete sentence? Damnation, he was so much better with paper. Put a quill in his hand and a sheet of paper before him, and he could eventually come up with words that seemed as if someone with a brain had written them.

Playing with the fabric of her skirt, she said, "Should I go?"

"What? No."

"Are you certain? You do not seem of a mind to converse."

"No, I—" Desperately, he racked his brains. She couldn't leave. "Let us talk of…" A sudden thought hit him. "Your employment. Let us talk of the law."

Her face drained of expression. "Your Grace?"

Bloody hell, he'd said the wrong thing. "The

law. You said... You wrote of it in your letters. With interest. Passion."

Face pale, she looked at him.

He cast about for things to say. "You said you'd learned of estate law through your scribing. You said you had scribed for an interesting estate? The one with the missing heir?"

"The Rogers-Wyndham estate," she said.

Relief flooded him. "Yes, that was it. Did they discover the heir?"

She shook her head. "It's all moot, anyway."

"Why?"

"I think there's another heir, one with a greater claim. The will specifically names a great-niece in Scotland, but the lead solicitor believes her claim to be invalidated by a codicil." Animation entered her face as she spoke. "The problem is the codicil has been worded in such a way that either stance could be taken, and the intent has been lost. There is a letter from Rogers-Wyndham that could clarify matters, but Mr. Hargraves will not even look at the letter—"

"Mr. Hargraves?"

Disgust darkened her features. "The lead solicitor."

"Oh."

She then proceeded to launch into a damning indictment of this Hargraves. Edward wasn't certain of the particulars, and her speech descended into legal technicalities he could not hope to follow, but her love of the law shone through.

"Why do you not say something?" he said when she paused.

She made a face. "Lord Beecham does not wish to hear from me. It's only through grace and good luck I'm even peripherally involved in the profession."

"Your position is tenuous."

"Yes. Of course." She smiled bitterly. "I am female. It is an offence to Lord Beecham I continue to be employed, and so I make sure he does not often encounter me. Then he can pretend I don't exist."

"And I have made him aware of you."

"Yes." She lifted a shoulder. "But you weren't to know."

He should have known. *Bloody hell.* He *should* have. That hadn't been his intention. He had made her life precarious when all he'd wanted... He'd just wanted to talk with her. To see her expression as she said the things she thought, to know what colour her hair, what shade her eyes. Well, now he knew her hair to be a light brown and straight as a pin, and when the wind picked at it, it became a halo around her head. He knew her eyes were grey, the same grey as the sky and just as changeable. He knew these things, and all this knowledge cost was increasing her uncertainty in her employment.

Well, he would fix it as best he could. "If there is trouble, you will tell me."

A strange smile twisted her lips. "And what will you do, Your Grace?"

Ignoring her sarcasm, he straightened and adopted his most ducal expression. "They will not refuse the Duke of Sowrith."

"No." Another bitter smile. "However, I am not the Duke of Sowrith."

"But you will have his support, and that is the same. Hear me on this." Catching her gaze, he did not waver. "You have no need to worry again."

The bitterness bled from her expression. Grey eyes captured him, drew him, and he willed her to believe his resolve and his dedication. He would not waver.

"Thank you, Your Grace," she said quietly.

The air thickened between them. His fingers twitched, wanting to cup her face and draw her mouth to his. He wanted to mark that freckle at the corner of her mouth with his tongue, learn the taste of her skin. He wanted to feel her body against his, her softness cradling him as he speared his fingers into her hair, destroying the tightly coiled bun. He wanted to claim her mouth with his.

"Why did you write me?"

The quiet words gave him a degree of control. "I beg your pardon?"

Her tongue darted out to wet the plump flesh of her lower lip. "Why did you write me? Why did you write those letters?"

Stifling a groan, he cursed himself. *Control yourself, man.* "You were the one who made the error."

"Yes." Steadily, her gaze kept his. "But you didn't need to write back."

No, he hadn't. Her letter had clearly been an error, addressed to her friend and full of the easy conversation of long acquaintance. He never should have read it, but he couldn't help himself. It had been so full of life, so happy and joyous, and he'd wanted to experience that. "Because I liked them. Your letters."

"What did you like of them?" A smile lit her face, a soft thing that seemed directed more at herself than him. "It was Etta, correct? She and her antics?"

A smile tugged at his own mouth, and he allowed it some expression, but not enough to pull his scar. "No, I liked you. That is, I like you." Heat rose along his neck.

"Oh." A similar blush stained her skin. "Well. I like you, too."

He couldn't stop his smile then.

She drew in her breath.

Immediately, he wiped the expression from his face. He knew how he appeared when he forgot himself.

She frowned. "Why did you stop smiling?"

Staring at the floor, he said, "I apologise. I know it's grotesque."

"What is grotesque?"

He dug his hands into the chair. "When I smile."

"No. Edward, no—"

"Of course it is," he said, and not even her calling him by his given name again lightened him. "I am scarred, Gwen. You cannot claim not to have noticed."

"No, I have. I only—You smiled, and I thought... You are so handsome, and when you smile, you are even more so—" She cut herself off. A furious blush lit her cheeks.

She thought him handsome? A low boil started within him, and he could not tear his gaze from her lips.

The air between them grew heavy with some kind of meaning. Body hardening, his hands prickled with the need to feel her skin beneath his touch. He needed to do something; he needed to distract— "Will you walk with me tomorrow?"

Looking somewhat dazed, Gwen blinked. "Pardon?"

Clearing his throat, he said, "It will be safer if you walk the moors with me."

"Safer?"

"I shouldn't like it if you break you head, not when you could have an extra eye looking out for you."

"Eye?"

"Yes. Just the one." He tapped the temple at the side of his good eye.

Her eyes widened.

He knew why. He was surprised at himself. He didn't think he'd ever referred to his injuries with such casualness before.

With a grin, she stood and bounced a curtsey. "In that case, Your Grace, I would be delighted to walk with you tomorrow. A girl could always use an extra eye."

Standing also, he barely winced at the pain in his hip. "Until tomorrow."

Still with a wide grin, she bobbed her head and then turned to leave. As she passed the bookshelf, she took a Gothic and waggled it. "For later."

Smiling, he shook his head. "Good night, Miss Parkes."

She hesitated. "You may call me Gwen. If you like." A furious blush blazed her cheeks.

His ears felt warm. "I may?"

"Yes." She took a breath and lifted her gaze to his. "May I call you Edward?"

Silent, he nodded. She offered a hesitant smile and then departed. He watched her leave then, suffused with a feeling of intense happiness, he sat in the chair and smiled at the fire.

Until tomorrow.

Chapter Five

SHE WASN'T HERE YET.

Edward glanced at the grandfather clock in the foyer. To be fair, it wasn't precisely eleven o'clock, and he had been in the hall for a good ten minutes. Gwen wasn't late, wasn't even remotely so. And yet he couldn't stop himself from glancing at the clock.

Exhaling, he forced himself to shift his regard elsewhere. Thinking better of it, he turned his body so the clock was on his blind side. Maybe if he had to physically move himself he would cease the constant time checking. He tugged at his sleeves, adjusted the length of his waistcoat, and then he had to force himself to cease that, too. This was ridiculous. He shouldn't be so...unsettled because he was to spend the day with Gwen.

Gwen. He rolled her name, the name she had given him leave to use, around in his mind. In the letters she had written her name, all versions of it. *Miss Parkes. Gwendolyn. Gwennie.* His lip quirked at the last. In her letters, she had spoken of her dislike for that permutation, and yet he could understand why her friend Etta would use it. Gwen would become exasperated by its use, and yet she would be delighted by the affection behind the diminutive. Just as he was delighted she'd invited him to call her by her familiar.

Heat rose on his skin, and he cursed himself. Damnation, when had he become so easy to fluster?

The grandfather clock in the hall started to chime, signalling the change of the hour, and a sound drew his attention to the stairs. Hand trailing along the balustrade, Gwen descended, her gaze arrested by something to the side.

Hands tightening behind his back, Edward battled the strange feeling swelling within him, an emotion that felt too large for his body to contain. A kind of roil began in his stomach, a mix of excitement and uncertainty and God only knew what else.

Willing his stomach to settle, he followed the line of her eye. He could see nothing of interest, but then he'd walked this house all his life. What seemed normal to him could seem odd to her. A smile tugged at him. It seemed that happened often since her arrival.

He moved to greet her, and she transferred her gaze to him, a wide grin on her face as she stopped on the second to last stair. "Did you know there's a gargoyle over that door?"

The stairs gave her height, making her gaze level with his. He glanced at the door she mentioned, and a hideous creature grinned down at him. As expected, what was normal to him was strange to others. "Yes."

"A gargoyle. Indoors." Grin still wide, she shook her head.

He didn't know how to answer, and so instead he offered his arm, the good one. Her fingers slid over his coat sleeve, curling around his forearm in a firm grip. The feel of her sent heat spiralling through him, tying his tongue. Damnation, why could he not say anything when he was with her? "Did you wear sturdy shoes?"

Her brows shot up. "Of course."

"Good." Leading her from the house and across the driveway, he cursed himself. Of course it was when he finally managed to speak, it would be to blurt inane questions.

As they walked, the familiar sights of Sowrith wrapped around him. The unrelenting cloud of the sky. The dark grey of rock. The dull green of grass. Each step they took calmed him, reminded him of what he loved about Sowrith. About his home.

"Are we to walk in silence?"

Gwen. Gwen was beside him. Gwen, to whom it seemed he could not utter two words together. "No. We can talk."

A sunny smile lit her face, so bright he was dazzled. "Oh. Good. Although, I seem to have some trouble providing conversation."

Surprise made him look at her sharply. "You? You don't have any trouble If anything, I—" He shut his mouth before he incriminated himself further.

She raised her brows. "You…"

He'd put his foot in it now. "I am not the most...verbose of persons." His lips twisted. "Not in person, anyway."

Lifting a shoulder, she squeezed his arm. "Not everyone has to be. You say enough, when it matters."

The tips of his ears burned. Damnation. Clearing his throat, he asked, "How is your family?"

Her expression bled of animation. "Fine."

"Your mother is well? Your father?"

She shrugged.

"Your father has not had another episode?"

She shrugged again.

His brows drew. She'd not before been reticent to speak of her family. "Do you not wish to speak of this?"

"No, I— No." She sighed. "As far as I know, my father is well. Etta has not reported otherwise."

The ground was uneven, and he had to concentrate on his gait before he could answer. "Your mother still does not communicate with you?"

"She thinks she's shielding me, that my life will be easier without knowing his condition." She exhaled. "I'm hoping to visit them soon, and then I'll know for myself his condition and hers. Neither of them is young anymore."

He remained silent a moment, pretending he was again concentrating on his gait. Eventually, he said, "At least you will know. And that will be good."

She nodded. "At least I will know."

Silence fell as they walked, broken only by the wind. For miles before them the moors stretched, broken by the jut of rock as if the earth was offended by the unrelenting reach of the grey sky. Behind them, Sowrithil would be a speck, a tiny man-made break in the wildness of the moors. The wind was not as harsh here in this shallow valley, merely threading gentle fingers through his hair rather than dragging it from his skull.

Edward drew them to a halt. This was his favourite of spots, the babbling stream at the base of the valley thin enough to step over easily, but fulsome enough to provide a rush of sound. "I love the moors."

He could almost feel her eyes upon him. "I love

the greyness of them, the harshness. The way they roll forever as far as one could imagine in a sea of dark grey and green, an endless voyage." The sky changed to a darker shade as the sun ducked beneath another cloud. "Your eyes are grey, a million shades of it."

He heard her draw in her breath. Almost reluctantly, he glanced at her. Grey eyes wide, she regarded him with surprise and something that approached fascination and...and...

He hunched his shoulders. "What?"

Without a word, she shook her head.

Bravado was the only solution. Squaring his shoulders and improving his bearing, he demanded, "What?"

"You say such..." As if in disbelief, she shook her head again. "There is such beauty in your words."

She'd robbed him of what little speech he had.

"It's like your letters, Edward. You say such things of beauty, and I don't know...I don't know how to respond."

Shoving his hands in his pockets, he wished himself anywhere but here.

"No, don't do that." Frustration made her words sharp. "Don't stop. It's amazing. You're amazing. I'm not... I don't mean it like..." She exhaled forcefully. "I don't know what I mean." Her gaze searched him. "Why can you write such things, Edward? How?"

Hands balling in his pockets, he shrugged. "It's paper."

"And that is different?"

"Of course it is."

"But here just now. You were telling me these things."

Yes, he had. He didn't know... "It was different."

"How?"

"We're here on the moors, and I—" Words stuck in his throat. Damnation, why wouldn't they come?

"Edward." Her hand slid up his lapel. Turning, he found her grey gaze upon him, a faint crease between her brows. "What is different?"

He stared into her eyes. She met his monocular gaze, no part of her expression revolted by the eye patch, the scars. He glanced at her hand, stroking his chest almost absently, her attention fully and totally on him. "When I received your letter, the one meant for Etta, it was like a ray of light, a beacon through relentless grey, so I responded, and you sent your next letter, and they... You were so full of joy it bubbled out from the page and made me think perhaps I could experience it if only a little. You had Etta and your parents and your employment, and though all three annoyed you on occasion, you had such...illumination." His finger began a mad rhythm against his leg. "I've never had any of that. I've been here alone since the accident. I didn't go to Eton. I was too ill. By the time I was old enough to attend university, I was so far behind there was no point. I went to London for the Season, but... That did not turn out well." Memories of horrified stares assaulted him, the whispers and notoriety that had come with his foray into society. Forcing the memories away, he said, "So I came home and stayed.

"Then you sent me a letter. A bright, shining thing, and we corresponded, and I...I wanted to meet you. So I arranged it that Beecham brought you to Sowrith, but I never thought he would not tell you, that I—" He grimaced. "You know what happened."

"Then you arrived. You were here, and I couldn't... There were no words. So I stood like a fool and watched you, and I wished I had the words that came so easily by pen. You were just like your letters—bright and gold and glittering with your smile and your lightness, even when you frowned. And that was amazing to me. You are amazing to me. I wish I could...I wish I could tell you..." Finally, he looked at her.

Eyes wide, she stared at him, her chest rising and falling rapidly.

Shifting his weight, he averted his gaze. "I'm sorry. I shouldn't have said those things. I—"

A gentle finger against his lips stilled his words, and he remained silent as her hand slipped to cup his cheek. The ruined one. Emotion shuddered through him as he absorbed her touch.

"See? You say such things, and I can't..." Her thumb tracing his cheekbone, her other hand slid up his chest to crumple his lapel as she pulled. Following her direction, he leant down.

Tentatively, her lips brushed his.

Hardly daring to breath, he stood stock still as she hesitantly explored the shape of his mouth, her lips moulding to his with small stops and starts. Her tongue darted against his lips, and he shuddered, the sensation exquisite and overwhelming.

Wrapping his good arm around her, he urged her close. She came, her arms slipping about his neck as her lips opened under his. The wind tore at his hair and howled in his ears, his heart thundering in his chest. Her mouth was warm and eager, tasting of honey and gold. Of Gwen.

They broke apart and stared at each other.

Slowly, he brought his good hand to brush a lock from her face. She caught his fingers, her thumb caressing the back of them.

Watching the tangle of their hands, he said softly, "I'd always hoped it would be like this. With you."

She turned her head into the cradle of his hand. "Is that why I'm here?"

The tips of his ears heated as his tongue tied itself into knots once more.

She sighed. "You've disrupted my life, you know."

He traced her ear with his finger. "Does it make you feel any better that you've disrupted mine?"

A small smile flitted about her lips. "A little."

Warmth started in his chest. "Because you have. Immensely."

"Immensely?" The smile became a grin. "Well, that makes me feel much better."

He smiled in return and hoped the ruined thing his expression didn't disturb her. It didn't seem to. Her grin merely became brighter as the wind whipped around them.

All was silent for a moment, but her words bothered him. "I'm sorry."

Surprise lit her expression. "For what?"

"Disrupting your life."

Her expression bled of the grin. Now serious, she said, "Thank you."

He nodded sharply. "You will tell me if you encounter any trouble?"

"Yes." Her hand slipped into his and squeezed. "But let's not think of that now. It might never happen." She leant into him, her head fitting into the hollow of his shoulder.

Wrapping his arm about her, he stared out over the moor. No, he would not think of such things, for they meant there might be a time when she was not near.

Chapter Six

EDWARD STOOD AT THE base of the stairs. Shoulders relaxed and without a cane, he stood with his head turned as if examining the panelling on the wall before him.

Hand trailing the balustrade, Gwen enjoyed the chance to simply look. Though ruthlessly pomaded, his hair still curled about his ears and tickled his collar, too long for fashionable society but perfect on him. The wind would whip it about him as they walked the moors, and she loved how it appeared when they returned to Sowrithil, a mad tumble of loose curls snared wild about his head. Now, though, it lay mostly tame and sleek along his skull, combed to hide the beginning of the scar on his left side.

The evening coat he wore was tailored to perfection, one of the suits he must have acquired during his brief stint in London. Black fabric hugged the broadness of his shoulders, outlined the slimness of his hips. His grey trousers clung to thighs powerful by walking the uneven moors, while the off-white waistcoat, shirt, and cravat contrasted with the unfashionable darkness of his skin. He spent much time outdoors and though the sun was often hidden behind cloud, his flesh showed a tan she had to admit she didn't find unattractive. Oh no, it was just the opposite.

He stood at the base of the stairs, seemingly careless and carefree, his bearing proud. He looked every inch what he was—a duke.

Her step faltered. Quickly, she recovered herself. It did not matter he was a duke. He was Edward, and that was all that mattered to her.

Glancing up, he saw her and he smiled, his careful smile, the one that didn't pull at his scar. The one that made her feel she was the person he most wanted to see in all the world. "Gwen," he said, and the pleasure in his voice sent a shiver through her.

She took the arm he held out, his right arm. "You look beautiful, Edward."

His cheeks turned ruddy. "Men aren't beautiful."

"Maybe men aren't, but you are. To me." She felt bold this evening, bold enough to say some of her thoughts as they occurred, and she thought him beautiful. He should know that.

Leading them to through the entrance hall, he said, "That should be my line. You look lovely, Gwen."

Now it was her turn to blush. She didn't have a choice of gowns, limited to the two she'd brought with her, but she'd worn the newer of the pair for this evening and had arranged her hair into a style Etta had once proclaimed flattering. She'd even woven a sprig of violets into her hair before removing it, deciding it was too fanciful.

The footman opened the dining room door, and Edward escorted her inside, helping her seat herself at the head of the table as surely great ladies did. Then, with his careful smile and a half-bow, he made his way to the other end of the table. The long table. She could barely see him at the other end, and they would surely have to shout if they wished to converse.

At the other end, Edward wore a frown. "Smith," he said, and the footman hurried to his side. They conversed in hushed whispers, then Smith hurried from the room. Next she knew, a veritable flurry of activity occurred. The placing was removed from before Edward while servants set a new one by her side, footmen moving the food from the middle of the table to be placed before her.

The dining table so ordered, the servants melted away, leaving only the footmen to wait silently for direction during the meal. With long strides only slightly hampered by his limp, Edward made his way to the place beside her.

Stunned, she watched as he seated himself. "Edward, is this at all proper?"

He unfolded his napkin. "Of course not, but it's just us, Gwen, and I have no desire to shout at you all night." He glanced at her. "You don't mind?"

"Oh, no." She glanced at the footmen. "Your servants won't think it odd?"

He shrugged. "It is not for them to think it odd."

Gwen ducked her head. Here it was, another example of the gulf between her and Edward. He thought nothing of the servants' opinions. No doubt he didn't even notice the six silent footmen stationed around the room, ready to carry out his slightest whim, while she…she was all too aware of them, of what they had to be thinking. She knew. She too had stood on the sidelines, silent and unseen.

"What are you thinking so hard about?"

Edward's expression was open, his pleasure in her company plain for any to see.

"Nothing." Criminy, she was a fool. She had no call to complain, not when Edward looked at her so.

They had worked most of the day, Edward sorting his legal correspondence and asking her opinion upon it. Though she'd reiterated again and again she was not a solicitor and could not give proper advice, Edward seemed to take all that in stride and counted her opinion worthy. She found herself making bolder and bolder pronouncements, and, toward the end, almost arguing with him about a particularly thorny part of estate law. He had not admonished her or made her feel her opinion was not wanted. They'd only parted as the dinner hour approached to dress for the evening. "How are you enjoying the new Gothic?"

Edward's features shuttered. "It is fine."

Gwen frowned. He'd received the book along with his correspondence yesterday morning. Before its arrival, the Gothic had dominated his conversation. The author was a particular favourite of his, and he'd been looking forward to devouring her latest tale. Gwen touched his coat sleeve. "Just fine?"

He wouldn't look her direct. "Do you truly wish to know?"

"Of course." She tugged his sleeve. "You like them, Edward. I want to know all about them."

The doors opened. Jerking her hand from Edward's sleeve, Gwen wrestled a sickly smile onto her face as the servants placed the first course before them—a clear soup smelling of beef and vegetables. As silently as they arrived, they departed.

Decidedly uncomfortable, Gwen shifted in her seat.

"Gwen?" Concern creased Edward's brow. "Are you well?"

Taking a breath, she forced a smile to her face. "Yes, of course. So this Gothic. What is it about?"

"I cannot think you wish to know. You said you didn't like them."

Truer words had not been spoken. The turgid phrasing and overwrought situations were not her cup of tea, but it was clear Edward enjoyed them, and that was what she cared about. "Well, I don't, but that doesn't mean I can't learn to like them. I've just not had the opportunity to read many."

A smile tugged at the corner of his mouth. "I cannot believe the daughter of a governess and a law professor did not find time to read whenever, and whatever, she wanted."

"Well, yes, I suppose when I lived with my mother and father, I could read whatever I wanted. But I've been in London for years now, and I don't have the time to read much besides law books."

"Why do you read law books? Do you need to?"

Criminy, such a question should not set her to blush. "No, I don't need to. I just...like them."

A black brow rose. "You like them?"

"I like you, too, you know," she said, however she was more than willing to rethink that particular state.

A grin burst across his face, so sudden it dazzled her. Stealing her hand, he rubbed his thumb over her skin. "And I am glad for it. However, you still read law books for fun."

"I'll have you know they broaden the mind." Trapping his fingers with her own, she tugged gently. "But don't go thinking I've not noticed you've deflected conversation from yourself, Your Grace."

Fighting a smile at his chagrined expression, she said, "Tell me all."

He heaved a sign. "Fine." Curling his hand into hers, he gently pressed the back against the cool wood of the table. "It's a new tale by Lord Christopher Hiddleston."

She tried to ignore how his touch sent shivers up her arm. "I know that name."

"You do? How? One would only know it if you enjoy Gothics. Which you don't"

Distracted, she said, "I know him."

"What?" Edward dropped her hand. "You know him? Lord Christopher Hiddleston? You know him. *How*?"

"He went to Cambridge. I think my father may have taught him."

"Lord Christopher Hiddleston. Your father taught him. This... I... You know Lord Christopher Hiddleston?"

Amused by his awestruck reaction, she said, "I don't know him well. Or really at all. I haven't seen him since Cambridge, and not since he published his Gothics. Etta knew him better than I. They would always argue."

"You— Etta— Bloody hell. Lord Christopher Hiddleston." He wiped his jaw.

Taking his hand, she tugged lightly. "So. Tell me of this tale."

Gaze on their entwined hands, he shook his head as his thumb smoothed the skin of her palm. "A young woman is orphaned by the death of her father and is sent to live at Ravenscar Manor with relatives she'd not known existed prior to her father's death. She stops in the village on the way, and the harbinger tells her of the legend—"

"The harbinger? There's actually a character called 'the harbinger'?"

"Of course not. That is the character's purpose. Besides, I forget his name." Brows drawing, he frowned so ferociously as to be completely unbelievable. "Don't interrupt."

She didn't bother to hide her grin. "Sorry, sir."

"As I was saying"—he gave her a meaningful look, to which she poked out her tongue. —"The young woman arrives at Ravenscar with the dread legend swirling in her head like doom. She—"

"What's her name?"

"Who?"

"The young woman. What's her name?"

"Does it matter?"

"No, not really." But it was so amusing to see him exaggerate his frustration at her interruptions.

Lifting his chin, he turned upon her what she imagined was his best ducal glare, the one that bade dire misfortune on any foolish enough to interrupt. "Anyway, this young woman has the legend in her head. *Longest night and darkest day, the lords of Ravenscar destroy all they survey. Only when white becomes black and gold turns to smoke will the lords of Ravenscar mend what is broke.*"

"I don't think that's correct grammar."

"Of course it isn't. It's a curse, but that doesn't stop our intrepid heroine from valiantly soldiering forward, braving Ravenscar and discovering its current lord, a dark and dangerous man."

A laugh bubbled from Gwen at that. Oh my, these Gothics weren't at all subtle, were they?

Edward ignored her. "Our heroine tempts her dark and dangerous lord, and before too long, they're sharing torrid embraces."

"Torrid? Really?"

"Have you never shared a torrid embrace?"

"Not with a dark and dangerous lord."

Edward's features became foreboding. "Then come to me, my petal, and we will share an embrace that will rock the heavens with its passion."

Oh. Oh, criminy. That was...was... She burst out laughing.

A smile playing about his mouth, Edward leant forward. His fingers tangled with hers, his thumb beginning a slow stroke along the sensitive skin of her palm. "Gwen. Do you not think I could rock you?"

Abruptly, the breath left her body. His dark eye burned into her, that small smile somehow knowing. It seemed to say he knew how she would taste, and he would like nothing better than her flavour on his tongue.

Good Lord, he could rock her. So easily.

"Your Grace."

Gwen jumped. Pulling her hand from Edward's, she returned it to her lap and attempted to regain her breath.

"Yes, Dobson?" Frown now genuine, Edward turned it upon the butler.

Dobson gave no indication if he quailed before such a look. "Are you and Miss Parkes ready for the next course?"

"Yes. However, please bring it in and leave it. Miss Parkes and I will serve ourselves."

"Very good, sir."

Gwen waited for Dobson to leave before she said all-too-brightly, "Shall we walk the moors tomorrow? I feel there are simply a million places that need to be explored."

"Gwen." Edward reached across the table. "Do not be disturbed by the servants."

"I can't help it." Unhappiness, uneasiness swelled within her. "I am their equal, not yours."

"You, more than anyone, are my equal," he said, and in the fierceness of his tone, she heard his conviction.

He didn't understand. How could he? He'd always been a duke. "But not socially. I am a commoner, Your Grace."

Sitting back, he crossed his arms. "Don't allow my title to come between us."

Miserably, she watched as he shut himself away from her. *How had it come to this?* She had destroyed their dinner with her insecurities and her fears. She would have such a short time with him. This couldn't last, and she was ruining what little time she had. Leaning over, she laid her fingers against his jaw and gently turned his gaze to hers. "Let us talk of other things, Edward."

Hand tightening on his bicep, he regarded her steadily. "You are my equal, Gwen."

A burst of something pure and lovely rioted inside her. It was so very wonderful he believed that to the point where his conviction burned within him. Uncaring of the servants, she rose to place her mouth against his. His lips were warm beneath hers and quickly turned eager. Taking control of the kiss, his fingers slid into her hair to keep her still for his tongue. She welcomed him, desire a delicious curl in her belly. His thick hair slid between her fingers and she could taste the wine he'd consumed.

Pulling back, he rested his forehead against hers. "Walk with me tomorrow?"

Hand curled around his wrist, she nodded. His scent washed over her, clean soap and the faintest hint of— "Does your valet pack your clothes with rosemary?"

Pulling back, he blinked. "I don't know. Why?"

"No reason."

Shaking his head, he sat back in his seat, but didn't let go of her hand.

Losing herself in him, she dismissed all thoughts of the servants lined silently against the walls. Who cared what the servants thought? She had Edward, and that was all that mattered.

Chapter Seven

EDWARD'S STUDY DOOR WAS a sturdy affair, built of solid oak. It was plain, having held its place for hundreds of years, most likely installed back when Sowrithil was Sowrith Hill Keep, a castle built by Edward's ancestors to keep out the Saxon rabble.

Hand resting on the dull brass handle, Gwen stared at the centuries-old wood. Darkness surrounded her, kept at bay only by the flicker of the lamp she held. Edward had told her the tale of his family as they'd sat on the moors and watched the sky change into a thousand shades of grey. He'd spoken first of the lords of Sowrith, and then the dukes, the line stretching countless generations and tracing back almost to the Conqueror. Then, with the half-smile he affected so it did not pull his scar, he'd told her his own tales of the stalwart knights and adventurers he'd imagined as a child seated in these very spots, his ruined leg speaking true of how he could never match thought to deed.

Exhaling, she bowed her head. She had stood before this door for at least five minutes, staring at the wood. Why was she hesitating? Every night for a week, she'd met Edward in his study. Every day, they'd walked the moors, Edward showing her his favourite places, and he'd become increasingly verbose, demonstrating his way with words with greater frequency. They'd spent each and every day together, and each and every day was better than the one before it. Each and every day, she found more qualities about him to like and admire.

So why, now, was she hesitating?

Squaring her shoulders, she shook off the ill feeling and turned the handle. The door opened silently, revealing the study lit by a merrily burning fire. Edward sat before it, his bad leg stretched in front of him on the chaise as he massaged his thigh. The chaise had not been there a week prior, moved in deference to their desire to sit as close together as possible.

Some small noise must have given away her presence for he turned, his face lighting when saw her. "Gwen."

Any uncertainty disintegrated in the light of his gaze, and the joy bubbling inside her threatened to burst. "Edward."

Cheeks ruddy, he ducked his head as he rose from the chaise, obviously still not used to her familiarity. Before she quite knew how it happened, she was before him. She wanted to embrace him, to wrap him in her arms and rest her cheek against his shoulder. She wanted to feel every part of him against every part of her. Edward, it appeared, seemed not quite sure how to greet her either, his hands raising and then falling.

Oh, but this was ridiculous. Throwing her arms about him, she buried her face in his neck, grazing his skin with her lips. "Hello."

He cupped the back of her head, holding her to him for a moment longer before they broke apart. "Hello."

Taking his hands, she led him to the chaise, pulling him down to sit with her. "What have you been doing?"

Brushing a lock of hair from her cheek, he gave her his half-smile. "In the hour and a half since we parted? Sitting in front of the fire, massaging my leg."

"Sounds exhilarating." Quite deliberately, she raised a brow.

His lips twitched. "Don't."

"What?" Pretending she had no clue what he was about, she maintained the imperious look.

"It is not amusing when you attempt to imitate me."

"No? Then why are you struggling not to laugh?"

Adopting his own imperious expression, he looked down his nose at her. "I do not struggle. I am a duke. If I wish to laugh, I will do so."

"Ah. I am sorry, Your Grace. I should not presume as to your emotions."

He nodded. "Quite."

She hit his shoulder. "Idiot."

He smiled, a wide smile where he forgot to disguise his scar. Raising her hand, she cupped the left side of his face.

He flinched.

Gently, she combed the loose strands above his ear, her thumb tracing the line of his hair. He tensed under her touch, but he didn't protest. Growing bolder, she traced the scar that cut his cheek, her thumb running along his strong jaw while her fingers trailed the network of scars down his neck. "Does this pain you?"

His good shoulder rose and fell, though he kept his eye fixed somewhere beyond her.

She traced the cord of his eye patch. "If you— Would—" Taking a breath, she collected her thoughts. "Can I see?"

For the longest time, he didn't respond. Then he gave a sharp nod.

Carefully, she lifted the patch. Where his left eye should have been were instead a sunken mass of scars, the eyebrow above cut by the thick scar snaking from his brow. She couldn't even begin to imagine the pain he'd endured. Chest a burn, she feathered the lightest of touches over his eyebrow. Jaw tense, his right eye remained resolutely forward.

Leaning forward, she placed a gentle kiss on his ruined eye socket. He sucked in a breath. She kissed his brow, his cheek, her fingers following the scar, the burn in her chest intensifying with every touch.

His thumb drew along her cheek, collecting the moisture he found there. "Don't cry, Gwen. It's long past."

She hadn't even noticed she was. "Edward..."

He kissed her cheek, her brow. "Don't."

Fingers drifting to his cravat, she bowed her head. The web of faint white scars disappeared beneath the fabric. Deliberately, slowly, she unknotted the cravat. He sat under her ministrations, his hand falling from her to the cushion of the chaise. Gauging his reaction with every movement, she pulled the fabric from his neck and spread the collar of his shirt, resting her touch on the bared skin of his throat. His fingers dug into the cushion, but he didn't protest.

Scars speared along his shoulder and down

what was revealed of his chest, thick, ugly scars that marred his skin and spoke of so much pain. Playing with the first of the buttons on his waistcoat, she gave him time to stop her.

He didn't.

Unbuttoning his waistcoat, she pushed it from his shoulders. A gentle tug separated his shirt from the waistband of his trousers and he bent his head to allow her to draw it from him. The moment the fabric cleared his head, his gaze returned to that spot ahead.

She turned her own to the scars. They riddled the left side of his body, a network of deep purple, angry red, and palest white. She traced the thickest of them and swallowed the lump that rose in her throat.

His jaw tensed. "They said I wouldn't walk again. That I'd lose my arm."

Lord. Lord God. Tentatively, she ran her hand over the arm they wanted to take, his muscles jumping beneath her touch. "Why—" She swallowed. "Why didn't they?"

"I wouldn't let them."

"How old were you?"

"Twelve."

Twelve. He was twelve, and he'd made them listen. "You made them do what you wanted?"

A muscle in his jaw twitched. "The accident made me the Duke of Sowrith. They had no choice."

Unable to stop herself, she traced the wicked-looking scar curling along his chest. His flesh jumped and tensed under her touch. Leaning forward, she placed her lips against the heavy twist of scars at his shoulder.

He drew in his breath. She rubbed her cheek against his abused skin and felt his fingers weave through her hair to gently cup her head. Curling her hand around his upper arm, she placed kisses along the scar beneath his collarbone.

Looking up, she found his gaze upon her, his dark eye glistening. A gentle curl of fingers bade her raise her face to his and another brought her lips to his. He kissed her slowly, sweetly, with all the passion and emotion hidden by stilted words and uncertainty.

Breaking the kiss, he exhaled, a soft smile playing about his mouth. Sitting there, half naked with hair mussed by her fingers, he didn't look a duke. He looked like...like Edward.

Pulling from him, she brought her fingers to the buttons lining the front of her bodice.

His eye widened. "What are you doing?"

She undid the first button, then the second. She couldn't answer him. If she thought about it, she would stop.

"Gwen?"

Criminy, what *was* she doing? She only knew she wanted to be as close to him as possible, to show him her vulnerability as he'd shown her his. What matter why she did this? It was for Edward, and he was beloved.

Leaning forward, she brushed his lips with hers as she shrugged out of her bodice, letting the garment fall to the ground where it may. As she was the one who laced herself into it, her corset was an easy affair, and with the busk unhooked and the constriction removed, she sighed against his mouth.

Warm hands curled around her shoulders and she watched as, slowly, his eye drifted down. All that remained between his gaze and her flesh was her chemise, flimsy and threadbare from repeated washings.

He swallowed, his grip tightening on her shoulders.

Gaze locked upon him, she started to unlace the thread holding her chemise closed only to be stilled by his palm spreading against the skin exposed by the gaping vee. She gasped, her heart beating madly, a gasp that turned into a moan when he ran his fingers beneath the fabric's edge.

Tugging his head to hers, she covered his mouth with hers, her tongue tracing the seam of his lips. With a growl, he jerked her to him, her breasts flattening against his chest, and she gasped at the feel of his skin against hers, her nipples pebbling as they brushed against the light smattering of hair on his chest.

The taste of smoke and brandy flooded her, then the taste that was Edward, that indefinable flavour she was coming to crave. His kiss, his touch, were driving her insane, his warm flesh against hers, his hardness against her softness.

She shifted in his lap, wanting closer, and he obliged, his hands gripping her as he manoeuvred her over him, her legs straddling him. His lips trailed down her neck, down the exposed skin of her chest, and then back to lick the hollow of her throat. Arching her neck, she moaned as his tongue flicked against her again. Oh lord, oh God, she wanted more, she wanted everything—

"Your Grace?"

Gwen froze. Beneath her, Edward tensed. "Dobson."

"Will there be anything more, Your Grace? Mrs. Horcastille and I would like to shut the house for the evening."

Edward's spine was ramrod straight, his

muscles still tense. "No. Nothing further."

"Very good, Your Grace." The quiet click of the door latch signalled Dobson's departure.

Abruptly, she became acutely aware of every part of her exposed skin, her shocking lack of dress. Wrenching herself from Edward, Gwen stumbled to gather her corset and bodice from the floor, struggling to pull her chemise back over herself. Her face felt as if aflame and her body hot, alternating with the sick, cold lump congealing in her stomach. What had she been thinking? That was...It was... She hadn't been thinking, not at all. She was cavorting—*cavorting*—with a man not her husband or even her fiancée. A man who was so far above her in consequence that the thought of a union between them was laughable...

"You'll hurt yourself."

She stopped in the middle of wrestling with her corset.

Posture correct, Edward seemed oblivious to the fact he remained half-naked. He gestured with his good hand. "The way you're putting that on. You'll hurt yourself."

Abandoning the corset, she crossed her arms over her chest. "He knew I was here."

Edward didn't move. "It doesn't matter if he did. He won't say anything."

"But he knew I was *here*."

"He won't say anything."

She needed to cover herself. Pulling at her bodice, she wrapped herself in fabric. As she did so, Edward looked down at himself and, shoving to his feet, he snatched up his shirt.

Arms tight about herself, she watched as he shrugged into it. She didn't have it within her to comfort him, to assure him she thought little of his scars beyond the pain they'd caused him. Not now. Not with this shame swirling within her. "He *saw* me, Edward. He saw me unclothed and…and…" She'd been draped over Edward, her chemise falling from her shoulders, his mouth against her skin, and she'd been *caught*.

"How do you think I feel?" Rigid, he stood with his shirt hanging open, his hair disordered, pain and tension scoured deep in his face. "Dobson has known me since *birth* and he— I—"

"But you are a duke. It doesn't matter what you do because you can cow anyone into thinking it normal."

A muscle ticked in his jaw. "Do you truly believe that?"

She tightened her arms. "Your word is law. You made the doctors keep your arm, and you were *twelve*."

His face bled of expression, and he was again the impassive duke she'd encountered upon her arrival, his thoughts and emotions hidden from her. Turning his back, he regarded the fire.

Miserable, she averted her gaze. How had they gotten here? Only moments ago, it had been excitement and heat, and she'd just wanted to be with him. Now, for the first time since their first days, awkwardness and distance stood between them.

He still stood with his back to her, his hands held tight at his back. "Perhaps I should go." Back to London. Away from temptation and ruin.

Away from Edward.

His shoulders tensed. "Perhaps you should."

Pain sliced through her. Telling herself it was for the best, she clutched her bodice tight. "Good night."

He didn't even turn. "Good night."

Gwen only half-remembered the journey to her room. Once inside, she sagged against the wood. She'd thought she could do this. She'd thought she could be bold and brave and unconventional, but all it took was almost getting caught by the butler to bring that delusion crashing down.

She'd asked herself what she was doing, and now she knew. Playing with fire with a *duke*, no less, and heading straight to ruin.

What was to come of this? No matter which way she looked at it, it could only end badly. She had parents to consider, a sick father and a mother who wouldn't admit she needed help. She had a precarious position at the chambers to maintain and a whole life that didn't involve an affair of the heart with a duke.

She needed to be sensible. She needed to let go of foolish fancies born of letters and time spent in a Dartmoor idyll.

She needed to let him go.

Chapter Eight

RIGHT ELBOW PROPPED ON his desk, Edward slouched in his chair. He knew he should straighten, that his posture should be as proper as his broken body could muster, but today, of all days, he thought he could be forgiven.

Exhaling forcefully, he rubbed his forehead. How could he have been caught with Gwen, half undressed and hands all over her? It was something a green boy would do, not a man of six and twenty, a duke for over half his life.

What added insult to injury was being caught by Dobson. The butler had known Edward all his life and, after the death of his parents, had become both mother and father. He'd sat with Edward during the fevers brought on by his injuries when he would accept no other's presence, had stood beside him when he'd taken his first faltering steps on his half-mended leg. It didn't matter Edward was a duke, that Dobson was his employee, his subordinate. All he could remember was the butler had known him from the time of his birth, and Dobson had caught him...with Gwen...

His eye-patch felt too tight. Hooking his finger under the string, he ripped it away and scoured the groove left behind. Gwen had been right to run, to escape his presence and his shocking lapse of judgment. It had been heaven to have her in his arms, to allow her touch, her kiss, to feel her skin against his. She'd seen his eye, had kissed his scars and made him feel somewhat normal for half a second.

And he'd repaid her with dishonour.

Digging his thumb into his brow, he traced the line. Dobson wouldn't say anything, not to Gwen. The butler would keep his counsel, would not intimate in any way to Gwen of what he had seen, but he would to Edward. With his very silence, he would condemn Edward's behaviour. With an impassive face, he would display his disappointment. But Dobson didn't know. He didn't know how Edward felt about Gwen, how he couldn't see a future without her.

He didn't know Edward loved her.

Heart racing, he straightened. He loved her? The thought had not crossed his mind before now. He'd simply enjoyed her presence in his life, in seeing her every day, in hearing her voice and seeing her smile. He'd loved her quick mind, the way she seemed to breathe the law, how she could absorb and interpret complex legal documentation and then discuss it with him in a way that was easy to understand.

Bloody hell. Of course he did. He loved her. He loved every part of her. He loved her passion for the law, her love and care for her family. He loved the way she described her London to him, her exasperation at her friend Etta. He loved the crinkle she got in her brow when she thought, her quick smile when her gaze first lit upon him. Her letters had made him half in love, and all it took was meeting her in person to fall the rest of the way.

Last night was badly done of him, and he would not allow it to happen again. He would court her proper, would make sure everyone knew his intentions honourable. Last night was done. He could not undo it, and so he would apologise and never again put her in a situation where she could be harmed. Then, they would go on their walk, and he would take her to the remains of the stone ring to the south of Sowrithil, the source of many a boyhood imagining. He would tell her of how he came to the ring often, imagined grand adventures of druids and pirates. Of course, adventures occurred only in his mind, his slow healing body preventing turning thought to deed, but Gwen would smile and ask questions and tell him tales of her own childhood. All would be as it was before.

Exhaling, he straightened in his seat, his leg and hip only protesting slightly. Placing his hands flat against the desk, he looked at the pile of work. He could focus. He *would* focus.

An envelope hidden mostly under other correspondence caught his eye, the script as familiar as his own. A letter. From Gwen.

Brows drawing, he nudged the letter from the others. Why was she writing him when she could easily come in the room and see him?

Perhaps she wrote an invitation. Perhaps whimsy had taken her, and she sought to put words to paper and then follow with action and deed. Perhaps she sought to invite him on an adventure, one that would take the place of all the adventures he could not have when he'd been growing.

Setting his jaw, he opened the letter. He refused to think it bad news. Life was made up of light and dark, and he could bloody well start to believe in the light.

Unfolding the paper, he read the first line.

Dear Edward, she wrote. *I have left.*

A roaring started in his head.

Maybe he had read it wrong. He read the line again. And again. And a fourth time, but the words and their meaning did not change.

Phrases jumped out at him, phrases like *I am a commoner* and *How can this work* and *I can't be bold and brave, no matter how much I want to.* Her father's illness and her mother's well-meaning lies were mentioned as well as the tenuous nature of her employment.

All of this meant only one thing to him. Gwen had gone.

He read the letter again. *Dear Edward*, she began—

Balling the paper, he threw it across the room and, for good measure, picked up a paperweight and hurled it at the wall. It crashed into the panelling, splintering in two.

Chest heaving, he stared at the ruined pieces lying on the floor. At least she felt she could use his given name, seeing as they were so far apart in consequence. At least she gave him the courtesy of telling him she was going back to London instead of leaving him to stand at the bottom of the stairs and wait for her appearance. And he would have waited. For her, he would have waited until he couldn't anymore, and then he would have sent a footman or a maid to search for her. When they couldn't find her, he would have suffered worry and panic and been convinced she had lost herself on the moor, had fallen and broken her head, and would not wake. So she had spared him that.

But this feeling in his chest could not be worse.

A sharp pain lanced through his left hand. Glancing down, he saw the two smallest fingers had curled into a ball, pressing into his palm, the ruined muscles protesting the tight grip.

He stared at his hand. Finally, he forced himself to relax. Shoving to his feet, he strode to the bell pull and tugged. Within moments, Dobson arrived. "When did Miss Parkes leave?"

Dobson blanched. "Early this morning, Your Grace."

"Did no one think to rouse me? Did no one think it odd she left at such an early hour? It's barely ten of the clock now."

"We were told Miss Parkes was to be treated as we would treat you, Your Grace."

"But you weren't supposed to let her leave!" Damnation, and now he sounded desperate. Gritting his teeth, he brought himself under control. Damn her to Hades, how could she do this? How could she just leave? "Did she take the carriage?"

Dobson nodded. "To Little Harrington."

Right, so if she left early this morning, it was possible she was still at the train station. If he rode, it was also possible he could reach her before she left.

If he rode.

He slammed his hand against the door. Bloody hell, his bloody scars wouldn't allow him to bloody ride. He was trapped by this body the accident had given him. The only time he had felt comfortable with his deformity was when she looked at him, when she'd touched him and kissed him and not seen his scars. For the first time, he'd felt almost…whole.

Then she'd left. She'd left, and she'd taken that with her as well as her smile and her laugh and her way of looking at him as if he were ridiculous, but she liked him anyway. She thought it funny that he was heir to this manse and yet read Gothic novels. She thought it grand that he made up stories of the moors in his head, and that the way he described them was poetic. She made him feel that perhaps he were more than the sum of his body that didn't work, more than the Duke of Sowrith.

"Your Grace?"

Dobson. He'd forgotten the butler's presence. Dobson hadn't responded at Edward's display of emotion, instead remaining impassive during his display.

In the face of such, Edward's shoulders slumped. Was he seriously going to chase after her like a fool? She had made her decision. "Please alert Mrs. Horcastille that we no longer have a guest."

Dobson nodded. "Very good, Your Grace," he said and then left.

Every muscle in his body aching, Edward made his way to his desk. She didn't want him. Lowering himself into his chair, he looked at the pile of correspondence. Gwen didn't want him.

Fine. If she wanted to leave, who was he to argue? He would not go where he wasn't wanted. He would remain as he always had, but with no Gwen to write to, no Gwen to kiss, no Gwen to love.

Gritting his teeth, he forced himself to pick up the report at the top of his correspondence, but before he'd read the first word, he slammed his fist on the desk. Damnation, he *would* argue with that. He was a bloody duke. She'd said it herself. He could do as he pleased. He'd kept his arm as a boy, and he'd bloody well keep her, too. He would formulate a plan, an argument to convince her, and he...well, he would convince her. He refused to let her go, no matter what her bloody letter said.

Shoving to his feet, he strode from the room, calling for Dobson. Now all he needed to do was brave London and the whispers and stares of society. But for her, he would brave much.

For her, he would brave anything.

Chapter Nine

GWEN STARED AT THE pristine whiteness of the page before her. Since her arrival at the chambers this morning at eight of the clock, the page had remained blank. Three hours had passed as she'd tried to distract herself with other tasks, had wasted a pot of ink and a ream of paper making mistake after mistake in her scribing, but the reason for her distraction would not leave her any time soon.

She'd left Edward.

Closing her eyes, she swallowed past the lump in her throat. How could she have left him in the way she had? At the time, it had seemed for the best to leave a letter on his desk and depart Sowrithil before any had risen, but it had taken only a day in London without him to admit the truth—she had run. Like a fool, like a *coward*, she had left without speaking with him, and why? Because it was easier. Because he would not have the chance to sway her. Because she could not bear it if he became upset...and she could not bear it if he didn't.

This blank piece of paper was to be her apology, but how could she write him? What could she say? It was like an ache, lodged beneath her heart and constant. A week. It had only been a week. How could she miss someone so badly after only a week? But then, it hadn't been only a week, had it? It had been a week plus all the months they'd corresponded, all the months she'd received his beautiful words and fallen a little in love without even having met him.

Gwen wiped at her cheek. Damnation, that way lay despair. It was over and done. Nothing could come of a courtship between a commoner and a duke.

Lifting her chin, she picked up the pen. She'd not heard from Etta in an age, and so she would write her. At least then the page would no longer be blank.

Dear Etta,
You will not believe the week I've had. I've been absolutely inundated with work—

A drop of water fell onto the still wet words, a perfect circle. The ink bled from the centre of the circle, distorting the words as it spread across the page.

Gently, she laid down the pen. She couldn't do this. She couldn't pretend she was well when everything inside her was twisted and close to breaking.

Taking a sheet of paper, she started a new letter.
Dear Edward.

Even seeing his name hurt. Biting her lower lip, she set pen to page.
I miss you.

What kind of fool began a letter with that? She scrubbed it out, the ink a scar upon the page.
I'm sorry.

That was even worse. Dropping her pen, she

cradled her head in her hands. She had no idea what to write him. After all their letters, after meeting him, after...after falling in *love* with him, how was it she couldn't think of a single thing to say?

"Miss Parkes." Lord Beecham's clerk stood in the doorway to her room, appearing decidedly unimpressed with his position.

Immediately, she cloaked her expression in polite enquiry. "Yes?"

"Lord Beecham requires your presence."

"Of course." Keeping her smile pleasant, she followed the clerk down the hall as her stomach tied itself in knots. The last time she had been summoned to Lord Beecham's presence, she had been informed she was to travel to Sowrithil. This would surely fare no better.

The clerk paused at the door to Lord Beecham's chamber. "Make sure you greet the duke correctly," he said as he rapped on the polished wood.

Gwen's head whipped around, but the clerk had already opened the door and, having done so, left.

Heart thundering, she entered the room. Lord Beecham sat behind his desk, his fingers steepled and displeasure drawing his features. At the window, his back to her, stood a man. A man who leant on his right leg more than his left, because it hurt his leg and hip to sit too long, and the carriage ride must have stirred his injury. His hands were laced because he wished to disguise the scars threading the skin as much as possible. He stared out the window because he didn't know how to greet people.

Because he was Edward.

Elation filled her, and confusion, and a tiny bit of anger. All three warred within her as she drank in his form.

"Miss Parkes." Lines of displeasure etched Lord Beecham's face, made deeper by her obvious distraction. "Miss Parkes, have you forgotten how to greet a duke?"

Her gaze slid back to Edward. The muscles of his shoulders had bunched, and his knuckles were white.

"Miss Parkes!"

With a start, she dropped into a curtsey, one awkward and ill-formed.

"Better," Lord Beecham said, a sneer evident in his voice.

"Do not speak to her so." Edward's voice was quiet, but it didn't disguise the command.

Lord Beecham blinked at Edward's back. "Your Grace?"

"You will speak to her with respect, Beecham, or you will not speak to her at all."

Astonishment rid Lord Beecham's expression of displeasure. "I beg your pardon, Your Grace, but I must insist I be given leave to treat those in my employ as I deem—"

"You will not speak to her so."

Silence, and then, "No, Your Grace."

Edward inclined his head sharply. "Beecham, there will be a change to our business matters."

A frown flirted with Lord Beecham's brows. "Your Grace?"

Edward turned. His gaze lit upon her, his expression giving no hint as to his thoughts. Gwen told herself she wasn't memorizing the curve of his lips or the colour of his eye, the way his hair fell about his face or the slash of his brow. "I will no longer deal with your solicitors," he said.

Lord Beecham paled. "Your Grace?"

Pain arrowed through Gwen. Edward was going elsewhere? She wouldn't even write him in a professional capacity?

"Miss Parkes and I are to marry, and, going forward, Her Grace will deal with all legal matters as pertain to Sowrith."

A roaring started in her head, and it seemed to her as if every muscle in her body had seized. This made no sense. None. How could he—And to just—

"Your Grace, this must be incorrect." Lord Beecham echoed her thoughts, his confusion evident. "Miss Parkes is not a lady."

"She will be, once we are wed."

"But...her birth is low, Your Grace. She is not... She is not..."

Edward's eye turned flat. "Do not insult my future bride."

"No, Your Grace, of course not. I apologise. I—"

"Not to me, Beecham," he said. "To Miss Parkes."

Beecham turned to her. "Please accept my apologies, Miss Parkes," he said, though every word sounded forced, and his expression resembled one who had just sucked a lemon.

Still dumbfounded, Gwen could only nod her acceptance.

Edward's jaw twitched. "Beecham, leave us."

"But, Your Grace—"

"Beecham. Leave us."

Lord Beecham looked from Edward to her and back again and, without further word, departed, closing the door behind him.

Gwen stared at the closed door. Criminy, who knew what he made of this? One thing was certain.

Her employment would not last the day.

"Hello, Gwen," Edward said quietly.

She recovered her voice as a kernel of anger lodged in her chest. Had Edward even *considered* what his actions could cause? "You're in London."

Pale and rigid, he nodded once. "Yes."

London, when he hated London. When he'd buried himself in Sowrithil and thought never to leave. London, to disturb her life on a whim. *Again.* "*Why* are you in London?"

"Because you left."

Her mind went blank. She could only stare at him, watching as he swallowed and took a step forward, the ducal tension melting from him as another sort took its place. "Gwen, you left, and I couldn't let you go. I *can't* let you go. I know you've concerns, but—"

"Yes. Concerns." She grabbed hold of the only thing that made sense. "Edward, you shouldn't *be* here."

"Of course I should." He set his jaw. "You left."

"My letter—"

A laugh barked from him. "Yes, let us talk of your letter. Damnation, Gwen. That's how you thought to leave?"

He was right. It had been a stupid thing to do. Crossing her arms, she clutched her biceps. "Why did you say we were to marry?"

"Because we are."

Anger flared, a spark she blew to a flame. "How did I miss this development? I would think I would remember a proposal."

"You asked where we were going. That. That's where."

In the letter. She'd asked that in the bloody letter. "How? You are a duke."

He scowled. "I *am* a duke. As a duke, I will marry whomever I please, and none shall have any say in it."

"Not even me?"

She'd stymied him, she could tell. Bitterly pleased, she continued, "You can't just announce that I'm to marry you without any preamble. Have you thought of the disruption this will create in my life? Yet again, you act with no thought of consequence. What am I to do when Lord Beecham discharges me, Edward? He will more than like not offer a letter of recommendation either. I deserve more than that."

"And what do I deserve, Gwen?" Recovering, eye blazing, he strode forward to within an inch of her. Refusing to back away, she stood her ground. "You left. You ran off and left a letter and—" Hands clenched, he took a breath, and then he looked at her direct. Her breath caught at the intensity of his single dark eye. "You left, Gwen."

This was all too confusing. Head throbbing, Gwen rubbed her temples. Marriage. There was no way this could work. The difference between them was too great.

Exhaling, he rubbed a hand over his face. "It was always going to be marriage, Gwen. I just hadn't formulated it in my head."

He didn't *understand*. "I'm a commoner, Edward."

Lifting his hand, he ghosted his fingers over her cheekbone. "It won't matter, Gwen"

"But it will." Turning from his touch, she stared at the closed door. "You saw Lord Beecham's reaction. None will accept it."

"I don't care."

A bitter laugh burst from her. "*I* care. I'll care every time someone cuts me, every time I'm shunned. It will happen over and over again, and it will be a hundred times worse than what I've endured here. Do you know they look through me, Edward? The solicitors all view me as an oddity, an unnatural female. The only one who doesn't is Mr. Davenport, and that's because I knew him when he attended Cambridge. Not to mention his wife likes me, and she'd be displeased if he treated me ill."

His hands clenched. "It won't matter."

"It *will*. What of the children, Edward? *Our* children."

Face hardening, he straightened. "Stop this, Gwen. Our children will be the sons and daughters of a duke and duchess. Anyone who treats them different will be made to know their error. These are excuses, and I will not have them."

This was how he'd kept his arm. This same tenacity enabled him to, at twelve years of age, stare down those so much older than him and force them to his will.

"Be damned to propriety and convention and what society thinks. I love you, Gwen. I love you, and I will not be kept from you because of what people I don't give a damn about think. You *will* marry me, and we will be happy. Bloody ecstatic, even. My place is with you, Gwen. I don't care about the rest."

He was magnificent in his anger, his chest heaving, his jaw set. How could she give this man up? How could she let society dictate who she loved?

It would be difficult. It would be conjecture and whispering and a host of people looking down on her. But in return, she would be with Edward. Married to

Edward. Sharing a life with him. How could she give that up?

Stepping forward, she grabbed his lapels and hauled him to her. Surprise flashed across his face as her mouth covered his.

His lips were soft with surprise under hers. Arm curling about the small of her back, he pulled her to him and, angling his head, he took control of the kiss. He delved deep, tasting her over and again as her heart thundered in her ears, as her hands slid into his hair and held him to her.

She couldn't give that up. She couldn't give *him* up. It would be hard, but easy wasn't worth much. She would learn to be brave, bold, and daring. She would do anything to be with him.

Breaking the kiss, he feathered his lips over her cheek, her jaw, and she felt in him his need as if he would die without her taste. Against his lips, she said, "My place is with you."

Such joy in his smile, so much it was blinding. "We shall be married at Sowrithil. Will you need much notice to move your things? Tell your family?"

Highhandedness. Again. "Edward, wait."

"I will arrange for your father to be brought comfortably from Cambridge to Sowrithil. He and your mother both. We will delay the ceremony to ensure they can arrive."

"Edward—"

"And, of course, Etta must be brought. You will want her as an attendant, no doubt. Do you believe—"

"Edward, I've not said yes."

He stopped, his head whipping to meet her eyes. "What?"

"You haven't asked. Ask me." She couldn't be

with him if he wouldn't ask. "Please, Edward. Ask."

Fingers tapping a rhythm on his leg, he said, "Gwen…"

"Please."

Jaw set, he locked his gaze with hers, and in his expression, she saw his fear. Oh, criminy. He was worried she'd refuse. "I won't say no."

Silence greeted her.

"Edward. Please."

He exhaled shakily. "Gwendolyn Parkes, will you marry me?"

Leaning forward, she touched her forehead to his. "Yes."

The most intense joy filled his expression. Cupping her face, he brought her lips to his, kissing her over and over and over.

Pulling back, she traced a pattern on his back. "I was writing you a letter."

Arms tightening, he brushed his lips against her temple. "Were you?"

She nodded, the fine fabric of his coat rubbing her cheek.

Gentle fingers beneath her chin raised her gaze to his. "What did it say?"

His eye was filled with such warmth. Such love. "It said *I miss you. Won't you let me see you again?*"

"I would have said yes."

A sudden wickedness filled her. "Would you like to know what else I would have asked?"

Expression wary, he said, "Yes."

"I would have asked to touch you. What would you have answered?"

Closing his eye, he swallowed. "Yes."

"And kiss you."

"Yes."

"And do wicked, wicked things."

A shudder racked him. "Yes."

"Shall I do them?"

He opened his eye. The love in his expression destroyed her and made her into something new. "Yes."

Epilogue

Blenheim Boarding House, London, 29 October 1847

Dear Edward,

My parents have written they will journey to Sowrithil via London and that they will stay here in London for a week before travelling with me to arrive at Sowrithil on the 2nd of December. Apparently, they are most anxious to meet you. Mama tells me she's not met a duke before, though Papa seems to think he's educated at least six, or rather, educated those who would later become dukes. In any event, I believe they are quite looking forward to rubbing shoulders with a peer of the realm.

Speaking of the wedding... Though I know he is not your favourite person, I think we should invite Lord Beecham. He did *give me employment, which led me to you. I am beyond grateful for that.*

It has been strange here at the chambers since you left. None but Lord Beecham knows of our engagement, but every so often, I will turn and someone will start as if caught in the act of examination. Rumour flies fast, and I am certain the employees here are aware of our connection. I will not be sorry to leave this place, and it only makes me glad I am able to practice law upon my arrival at Sowrithil. And, of course, I cannot wait to be your wife.

Speaking of such things... I have thought... Do you think we should build a school? A law school? For women?

I hope you have not expired of shock. I should like to see a place where women can study the law, and I feel certain it will be most popular. Education will do much to alleviate discontent and provide focus where there currently is none. I have discussed this with a colleague here in London, Mr. Davenport, who himself was witness to the terrific fights in which Etta and a gentleman of his acquaintance would engage. If Etta and I had attended a law school, we should not have been so passionate in our expression...

No. I cannot write such a blatant untruth. Are you smiling, Edward? Perhaps laughing? Can you imagine Etta and I unpassionate about the law?

However, back to the school. Papa believes it a progressive idea, one that has taken far too long to come to fruition. He said he saw many intelligent girls languish for lack of a school. Mama agrees and believes several other of the professors would be amenable.

Etta, of course, is in favour of a school.

However, I am desirous most of your opinion. Do you believe it a good idea? Should we attempt it? It will ruffle quite a few feathers, and we will face opposition from many sources. I feel it would be worth it, though, and in for a penny, in for a pound. If we are to cause scandal with our union, why not make it a scandal of such truly magnificent proportions they will remember it for a hundred years

to come?
  All my love,
  Gwen
  P.S. Etta has responded in the affirmative to attend our wedding. I am sure you are beyond thrilled to finally meet her. She threatens to dress as a serving maid so you should recognize her more easily.

***

Sowrithil, Devon, 8 November, 1847

Beecham,
  I write to remind you of my impending marriage. My future duchess has requested yours and your lady's presence at the ceremony, which will take place on the 17th of December in the chapel at Sowrithil. Do not fail to attend. I should dislike to see Her Grace upset.
  Oh, and Beecham? Do not address legal correspondence to me. You have been told Her Grace will be handling all legal matters. I will not correct you again.
  Sowrith

***

Sowrithil, Devon, 8 November 1847

Dear Gwen,
  I have written to Beecham as you have requested. Hopefully, he responds in the negative. Tell me if you feel any discomfort at the chambers. Beecham and I will have words.
  A school sounds a grand idea. What would be

required?

The sky was a bluer shade of grey today with the occasional threading of white. It will be the last time the sky is this colour before winter comes and paints everything in white. I was hoping to make it to our tor today to think of you and make plans of how I'll touch you when you return to Sowrithil, but instead estate business demanded I meet with tenants and thus my plans were lost. Maybe tomorrow I will sit and anticipate your return and how the ache inside me will ease when I hold you close.

I miss you,
Edward

P.S. Of course I shall recognize Etta should she dress as a maid. She'll be the insubordinate one, yes?

P.P.S. And, it almost goes without saying I cannot wait to be your husband.

***

Sowrithil, Devon, 2 March 1848

Lord Beecham,

I write to inform you His Grace and I have returned from our wedding journey. I note the correspondence from your chambers in regards to His Grace's estate planning and will forward appropriate documents and comments to your chambers shortly. In the intervening period, please forward a copy of His Grace's Last Will and Testament as his circumstances have now changed, and as such his Will requires updating.

Yours, etc
Her Grace, the Duchess of Sowrith

***

Sowrith House, London, 21 June 1848

Dear Edward,
It will be at least another week before I can come home. The solicitors are seeing fit to tie me in legal jargon until my eyes and ears fairly bleed.

The planning for the school fund goes well, though. I feel certain we will break ground before the spring. Etta is driving me insane with her notions of what should be included. She feels certain the curriculum should include Mathematics and Philosophy, though I have stressed those disciplines are not included in the current Schools of Law.

The roses at Sowrith House are blooming, a riot of colour against the unrelenting grey. I miss the greys of Sowrithil, the subtle changing light of the moors.

And, of course, I miss you.
All my love,
Gwen

***

Sowrithil, Devon, 30 June 1848

Gwennie,
If the solicitors are so keen to have you stay in London, then I shall come to you. As it is, you've been from me too long.

The sky was a stormy shade of grey today, one that reminded me of your eyes when you're vexed. With others, of course. I never vex you to such a state.
Your Edward

***

Sowrith House, London, 5 July 1848

My Edward,
There's no need to come to London. I know you dislike it. I feel certain this business will conclude soon, and I will depart London the very moment it does. As you say, I have been too long from you.

However, never vex me? What rubbish. Why, I'm fairly vexed with you three times an hour and double that on Sundays. Of course, you do have a way of charming me from vexation.

Soon. I promise.
All my love,
Gwen
P. S. You know I dislike Gwennie. Why must you vex me so? You're not even here to make it up to me in your charming way.

***

Sowrithil, Devon, 11 July 1848

Gwen,
Too late. I shall travel tomorrow and should be in London the following day.
Edward
P. S. I shall make it up to you. In my charming way.

P. P .S. Your friend Etta sent a letter with direction to Sowrithil. I have not read its contents, but feel certain it regards the school. I shall bring it with me.

***

Sowrith House, London, 15 July 1848

Dear Edward,
This letter will not reach you, seeing as you are already travelling to London, however, know that I shall await your arrival. And I shall plan wicked things.
All my love,
Gwen

Acknowledgments

Thank you to the amazing A.L. Clark for your support, your editing skilz, and the re-introduction to roller coasters. I'm sorry I am a soulless monster who found them meh. Also, we totes need to write the eerie, fish-out-of-water, gangster, star-crossed lovers Gold Coast TV show. I'm certain Netflix are dying for our call.

To TP and the small humans you made, you peeps are my found family. I'm so privileged to have you in my life.

To my biological-ie-we-share-DNA-or-have-married-into family, you are the best. I'm also super privileged to have won that particular crap shoot.

This book would not exist with the outstanding authors involved in the Common Elements Romance Project. There are so many amazing stories in this project, I highly recommend you check them out.

And finally, as always, to you, the reader. Thank you for reading RESCUING LORD ROXWAITHE and if you have five minutes, it would be amazing if you would leave a review.

Until next time.

Read the first book in the Lost Lords series

FINDING LORD FARLISLE

The boy she never forgot
Lady Alexandra Torrence knows she's odd. Fascinated by
spirits, she sets out to investigate rumours of a ghost at
Waithe Hall, the haunt of her childhood. Its shuttered
corridors stir her own ghosts: memories of the friend she'd
lost. Maxim had been her childhood playmate, her kindred
spirit, the boy she was beginning to love …but then he'd
abandoned her, only to be lost at sea. She never expected
to stumble upon a handsome and rough-hewn man who
had made the Hall his home, a man she is shocked to
discover is Maxim: alive, older…and with no memory of
her.

The girl he finally remembers
Eleven years ago, a shipwreck robbed Lord Maxim
Farlisle of his memory. Finally remembering himself, he
journeys to his childhood home to find Waithe Hall shut
and deserted. Unwilling to face what remains of his
family, Maxim makes his home in the abandoned hall only
to have a determined beauty invade his uneasy peace. This
woman insists he remember her and slowly, he does.
Once, he and Alexandra had been inseparable, beloved
friends who were growing into something more…but the
reasons he left still exist, and how can he offer her a
broken man?

As the two rediscover their connection, the promise of
young love burns into an overwhelming passion. But the
time apart has scarred them both—will they discover a
love that binds them together, or will the past tear them
apart forever?

Read an Excerpt from
FINDING LORD FARLISLE
Lost Lords, Book One

Chapter One

Northumberland, England, August 1819

LIGHTNING STREAKED ACROSS THE
darkening sky and thunder followed. Stillness held
sway a moment, the air thick, before a torrent of rain
battered the earth.

Wrestling against the wind, Lady Alexandra
Torrence tucked her portmanteau closer to her person
as she pushed determinedly toward the estate looming
in the distance. The storm had been but a sun-shower
when she'd set out from Bentley Close, her family's
estate only a half hour walk. While the light cloak she
wore protected her from the worst of it, the wet was
beginning to seep into her skin.

She pulled her cloak tighter. It was only a little
farther and she'd be at Waithe Hall, though there
would be no one to greet her. Waithe Hall had been

closed for years, ever since the previous earl had died. The new earl—Viscount Hudson, as he'd once been—resided almost exclusively in London. Her family and his had been close for as long as she could remember, their townhouses bordering each other in London just as their estates did here in Northumberland. The earl was her elder by nine years, and his brother Stephen by five, but Maxim, the youngest, had been but one year her senior and—

She stopped that thought in its tracks.

Before too much longer she stood before the entrance to Waithe Hall, and with it, shelter. The huge wooden doors were shut. She could not recall that she had ever seen them closed and locked. In the past when she'd visited the family had been in residence so she would walk straight in, calling for Maxim before she'd completely cleared the entrance—

Slowly, she exhaled. After a moment, she pulled the key from her pocket, the one Maxim had given to her for safekeeping when he was ten and she nine, so they could always find their way back in should the doors ever be locked—

Shoving the key into the lock, she blinked fiercely as she forced memory aside once more. She could do this. It had been years, the wound so old it should have long since faded. She could investigate Waithe Hall and its ghosts, and she would not think of him.

The key turned easily, the door swinging open. She stepped inside. Cavernous silence greeted her, the din of the rain that had been so deafening now distant. The entrance stretched before her, disappearing into darkness, and the storm had made the late afternoon darker than usual, swallowing any light that peeked through closed doors. Pausing mid-step, she wondered if perhaps she had made a mistake in coming here.

Shaking off doubt, she started through the hall. The rain echoed through the vastness, the hollow sound strange after being caught in its fury. Fumbling through her portmanteau she found a candle and tinder.

The flickering light revealed an entrance corridor that opened into an enclosed court encompassing the first and second floors and an impressive chandelier draped in protective cloth hung at its centre. Memory painted it with crystal and candles, and she remembered sitting on the landing of the second floor, legs dangling through the gaps between balusters as she and Maxim counted the crystals for the hundredth time.

Bowing her head, she cursed herself. She should have known she could not keep the memories at bay.

A roll of thunder reverberated around her, leaving behind quiet and dark. All her memories of Waithe Hall were full of life, the butler directing servants, fresh flowers in the vases lining the court, light spilling through from the mammoth windows. Now the windows were shuttered, and an eerie silence broken only by the sounds of the storm pervaded.

Hitching her bag, she made her way to the sitting room. It was as still as the rest of the estate, the furniture draped in holland covers, the windows also shuttered. Setting her candle down, she placed her cloak over the back of a chair and rested her bag on its seat, glancing nervously about. She caught herself. *Don't be stupid, Alexandra. There's none here.*

Before she could think further, she unbuttoned

her bodice. Her clothes were soaked, uncomfortably damp against her skin, and a chill was beginning to seep through, though it was the tail end of summer and the days were still mostly warm. She'd chosen a simple gown, one she knew she could get into and out of herself.

Heat rose on her cheeks as she shucked out of the bodice. There was none here. She knew there was no one. Cheeks now burning, she untied her skirt and petticoats, left only in her stays and chemise. She would love to remove her stays as well, but they were only slightly damp and she couldn't bring herself to disrobe more than she had.

Opening her bag, she pulled out a spare bodice, skirt, petticoats and, finally, a towel. Thanking her stars she'd had the forethought to bring it, she quickly swiped herself, chanting all the while there was no one watching her, that doing this in an abandoned sitting room was not immodest.

In record time, she'd managed to reclothe herself. Hanging her wet clothes to dry, she pushed her hair out of her face. Once she had explored further, she would choose one of the bedchambers as her base, but for right now the sitting room would suffice.

A thread of guilt wound through her. Technically, the earl did not know she was a guest of Waithe Hall—and by technically, she meant he didn't know at all. She was confident however, he could have no objection. She had been a regular presence at Waithe Hall when she was a girl, and the earl held some affection for her. She was almost positive. Maxim had often said his brother thought her—

Damnation. Bracing herself against a chair, she bowed her head. She had thought more of him in the last hour than she had in the year previous. It was this place. She'd managed to convince herself she no longer felt the sharp bite of grief, but she did. It struck her at odd moments, and she could never predict when. One would think it would have lessened with time, but it hit her fresh and raw, as if she bled all over again. She'd been a fool to think she would remain unaffected returning here—he was everywhere.

She closed her eyes as realisation cut through her. She was going to think of him. It was inevitable. However, she had come here with purpose and she would not allow this preoccupation to deter her.

The ghosts of Waithe Hall beckoned.

A darkening gloom shrouded the drawing room. Night approached, quicker than she'd liked, but she was determined to at least do a preliminary sweep of the estate to refresh her memory before it became too dark to continue. There was much to do before she camped out in the affected room one night soon, not the least of which was determining which room was affected.

From her bag, she pulled a compass, a ball of twine, and her notebook. Bending over the flickering light of her candle, she opened her notebook and dated the page, jotting down her notes on the expedition thus far.

There had always been tales of ghosts at Waithe Hall. On her and Maxim's frequent rides about the estate, she remembered listening wide-eyed as Timmons had told them tales of ghosts and woe. The groom had waxed lyrical on the myths and legends of spiritual activity at Waithe Hall, and she'd been completely fascinated. Maxim had never seemed interested, but he'd always followed when she'd concocted a new adventure to discover ghosts and ghouls. As an adult, she'd turned her fascination into a hobby, researching and cataloguing ghost tales at every manor and estate she'd attended. Her own family's estate held a ghost or two, stories her father had been only too happy to tell. She'd documented his tale and others, and had submitted several articles to the Society for the Research of Psychical Phenomena. They hadn't as yet chosen to publish any of them, but she was convinced if she persisted, eventually they would.

Then, four months ago, reports had crossed the earl's desk in London of strange lights at Waithe Hall. He'd mentioned it in passing to her father, who in turn, knowing her fascination, had mentioned it to her. He'd also issued a stern warning she was not to pursue an investigation but, well, she was twenty-five years old and in possession of an inheritance a great aunt had left her. Her father could suggest, but he could not compel.

The lights could be any number of things, but the report had contained accounts of a weeping woman, and the light had become a search light. Memory reminded her of a tale Timmons had told, the lament of a housekeeper of Waithe Hall who had lost a set of keys and caused a massacre. Her lips quirked. Timmons' tales had ever been grisly.

Determination had firmed and within a week she'd made her way to Northumberland and Waithe Hall. Bentley Close had been shut as well, but unlike Waithe Hall, a skeleton staff kept the estate running. Along with her maid, Alexandra had arrived late last night though she hadn't been in a position to set out for Waithe Hall until late this afternoon. Her plan had always been to spend a few days here, but the rain made it so she now had no choice.

She would rather be here than in London anyway. Besides pretending she was unaffected by those who called her odd, her younger sister had finally made her debut at the grand old age of twenty. Lydia was taking society by storm, determined to wring every ounce of pleasure out of her season, and she had confidently informed their parents she didn't intend to wed until she had at least three seasons behind her. At first horrified, their parents had resigned themselves to neither of their daughters marrying any time soon.

As the eldest of her parents' children and a female besides, she had borne the brunt of their expectations in that respect, but at least Harry had now brought them some joy. He and Madeline Pike were to marry next year, the wedding of the heir to a marquisette and a duke's daughter already touted as the event of the season. George had absconded to the continent, no doubt investigating the most macabre medical reports he could, while Michael was still at Eton.

Upstairs, a door slammed shut. Alexandra jumped, hand flying to her racing heart. It was the wind. It had to be. Even now it howled outside, rain pelting the roof and echoing through the hall as distant thunder rolled.

Hugging the notebook to her chest, she shucked off any concerns. There was no time like the present. She would start with an examination of the ground floor. The kitchens and servants rooms would take an age, so better to examine the family rooms and save the servants for another time.

The portrait gallery was as she remembered, a long stretch of hall that displayed the Farlisles in all their permutations. Quickly, she traversed its length, telling herself the dozens of eyes of previous Farlisles did not follow her, that they did not judge her an unwelcome guest. Cold slid up her spine and she moved faster, especially as she passed the portrait of the old earl and his sons, Maxim staring solemnly from the portrait.

Pretending she felt not a skerrick of unease, she noted the gallery's dimensions in her diary and moved on to the second sitting room. Again, nothing in particular was out of the ordinary.

The library was at the end of the corridor, and the door opened easily under her hand. It really was most obliging of the steward not to have locked any of the doors inside the estate. This room was vastly different to her remembrance. Few books lined the shelves thick with dust, and holland covers draped most of the furniture, although one of the high-backed arm chairs before the fire was lacking the covering. Peculiarly, one of the windows here was unshuttered, the weak light of storm-dampened twilight casting eerie shadows on the wall opposite.

She'd always loved the library and its two storeys containing rows upon rows of books. As children, she'd insisted she and Maxim spend an inordinate amount of time within its walls, happily miring herself in book after book. Maxim had always been bored within seconds, spending his time tossing his ever-present cricket ball higher and higher in the air to see if he could hit the ceiling two floors above. He'd even managed it, a time or two.

Sharp pain lodged beneath her breast. Rubbing at her chest, she took a breath against it, pulling herself to the present. Somehow, night had encroached upon the room. How long had she been stood there, lost in memory?

Moving further into the room, she trailed her fingers over the side table next to the undraped chair. A stack of thick books was piled high, the top one containing a marker. Why was there a stack of books? Had an apparition placed them there?

A prickle rippled along her skin. She'd never seen a ghost. She'd heard hundreds, thousands of stories, but she'd never— Steadying herself, she flipped open the book to the spot marked, noting it was a history of the Roman invasion and settlement of Cumbria. Sections and rows were underlined with pencil, writing filled the margins, and there was something about the hand....

Closing the book, she placed it back on the stack. Why was this here? Every other part of Waithe Hall she'd seen had been closed, shut away. This room held an uncovered chair, a stack of books and.... The fireplace held recent ashes.

Her heart began to pound.

Again, something—a door?—banged. Whirling around, she searched the encroaching dark, her gaze desperate as her chest heaved. What if the lights weren't a ghost? What if it was a vagrant, someone dangerous and unkind? What if...what if it were a *murderer*?

The agitated sound of her breathing filled the room. Getting a hold of herself, she reined in her imaginations. Her thoughts could—and frequently did—run to the extreme. Although these anomalies were curious, there could be a perfectly mundane reason for their presence. There was nothing out of the ordinary, besides the books, and the fireplace, and—

She took a breath. *Calm, Alexandra.* She was

purportedly an investigator. She would investigate.

The fireplace had without doubt been used recently. Newly cut logs placed in a neat pile to the side. Sconces held half-used candles, their wicks blackened and bodies streaked with melted wax. She could see no other signs of occupation—

Something banged for a third time, closer now, and brought with it a howling wind. Alexandra jumped, grabbing at the table for balance as the door to the library flew open, the heavy wood banging against the wall, the books wobbling and threatening to fall. Blood pounding in her ears, she looked to the darkened maw of the library's entrance.

An indistinct white shape filled the door, hovering at least five feet above the floor.

A scream lodged in her throat. She couldn't move, couldn't make a sound. She could only stare as the thing approached.

Lightning crashed, flashing through the room. She gasped, a short staccato sound that did little to unlock her chest.

Lightning crashed again. The shape became distinct in the brief flash of light, revealing a man dressed in shirt sleeves and breeches, his dark hair long about his harsh face. A strong, handsome face that held traces of the boy she'd thought never to see again.

Blood drained from her own face, such she felt faint. "Maxim?"

Chapter Two

"WHAT ARE YOU DOING here?" it—he— growled.

"Maxim?" she repeated stupidly. The apparition before her looked so much like Maxim...if Maxim had grown to a man, developed an abundance of muscle and four inches of height. It couldn't be Maxim...but if it were an apparition, why would he appear grown? When last she'd seen him, he'd been fifteen and skinny as a reed, not much taller than she. It couldn't be him.

Lightning lit the room once more. His shirt was loose about his thighs, the ties undone and the neck gaping open, his breeches smudged with dirt. All was well tailored and untattered. Surely, if he were a ghost, his raiments should be tattered?

The same chestnut hair fell over his brow, too long and ragged, while his face had broadened and hardened, his eyes were the same, chocolate brown under dark brows. He'd grown to a man, broad shoulders and ropy muscle apparent behind the scant clothes he wore, his breeches stretched over powerful thighs and strong calves, his large feet shod in well-worn leather boots.

He was supposed to be dead. Eleven years ago, he had abruptly left Eton and set sail on one of the Roxwaithe ships, bound for America. She'd been so confused at the time, and he'd refused to tell her why. Six months later, they had received word the ship had been lost at sea. None had survived.

With startling clarity, she remembered that day. Her father's face, careworn and concerned, as he'd told her. Her mother's worried eyes. The pain in her chest, frozen at first, until she'd excused herself, blindly making her way to her chamber only to stand in its centre, confusion filling her until she'd happened to glance upon his cricket ball, the one he'd given her the last time she'd seen him, three days before he'd left when he'd refused to tell her why he was leaving, and once she'd returned home she'd thrown it onto her dressing table, angry beyond belief at him, that he was going away, and then, then a great gaping hole had cracked open inside her and she'd slid to the floor, pain and grief and devastation growing inside her until it had encompassed all, it had encompassed everything and it hadn't stopped, it hadn't stopped, it—

It was eleven years ago. The pain had faded, but had never truly left. She'd thought she'd learned to live with it. But now…he was here?

A thunderous scowl on his face, he made a noise of impatience. "I do not have the inclination for this, girl. Tell me why you have come."

His voice crashed over her. That, too, had deepened with age, but it was him. It was *him*.

"It *is* you." Joy filled her, so big it felt her skin couldn't contain it. Throwing herself at him, she enveloped him in a hug.

He stiffened.

Embarrassment coursed through her. What was she thinking? Immediately, she untangled herself from him. "I beg your pardon," she stammered. Always before they'd been exuberant in their affections. They'd always found ways to touch one another, even though that last summer, the one before he'd gone away, she'd begun to feel...more.

Clasping her hands before her, she brought herself to the present. Much had changed, now they were grown and he, apparently, had not died.

Maxim had not died.

A wave of emotion swept her, a mix of relief, joy, incredulity.... It buckled her knees and burned her eyes. He was alive. *Maxim was alive.*

"When did you return? Do your brothers know?" she asked, steadying herself as she swiped at the wetness on her cheeks. "The earl is lately in London, but I'm certain he would return should he know. My father will be so pleased to see, as will my mother. George and Harry will be beside themselves, and Lydia and Michael too, though they were so young when—" She cut herself off, barely able to say the word *died*. "We mourned you, Maxim."

He came closer. He'd grown so tall. When last she'd seen him, barely an inch had separated them, but now he was at least two hands taller. Faint lines fanned from his eyes, the tanned skin shocking in the cold English weather. Wherever he'd been, it had been sunburned.

"I ask again," he said. "Why have you come?"

Confusion drew her brows. "Maxim? Don't you remember me?"

Starting at the blonde hair piled limply on her

head thanks to the rain, he ran his gaze over her. He traced her face, her throat, travelled over her chest, swept her legs. A tingling began within her, gathering low. She was suddenly aware of how her breasts pushed against the fabric of her chemise with every breath, of a pulse between her legs that beat slow, steady....

He raised his gaze to hers. Silence filled the space between them before, succinctly, "No."

It was like a punch to her belly. "It's me. Alexandra."

No reaction.

Oh. Oh, this hurt.

Lifting her chin, she managed, "I am Lady Alexandra Torrence, daughter of your neighbour, the Marquis of Strand. We grew up together."

His expression did not change.

"Your father, the previous earl, and mine were like brothers."

He stared at her. "Previous earl?" he finally asked.

"Yes," she said. "Your father passed away some years ago. Your eldest brother is now earl."

Again, no change in expression. Did he not care his father had died? But what did she know of this new Maxim? Less than an hour ago, she had not known he was alive.

He continued to stare at her. She fought the urge to shift under that flat gaze. "Why are you here?" he repeated, his tone harsh and impatient.

"I was—" Her voice cracked. Cursing her nerves, she cleared her throat. "I am investigating. The villagers spoke of a ghostly presence, lights and wails, and I...." She trailed off. Lord, it made her sound so odd. He'd always teased her about that oddness, and always with affection. She didn't know what this new Maxim would do.

Finally there was expression on his face. She wished it had remained stony. "Ghosts? You have invaded my home for ghosts?"

The disgust in his voice made her cringe. "To be fair, I didn't know you were here. No one did."

Expression still disdainful, he didn't reply.

Irritation pushed aside devastation. How could he not remember *her*? "This is not *your* home."

His brows shot up. "*That* is your argument?"

He sounded so much like *her* Maxim. They'd argued often, and the number of times he'd said those exact words, in that exact tone…. She shook herself. "Yes. It is."

"A fallacy. You argue a fallacy."

"It is not a fallacy. It is objectively true. Waithe Hall is the ancestral seat of the Earls of Roxwaithe. You are not the Earl of Roxwaithe, ergo, it is not your home." Knowing it was childish, she tossed her hair and glared.

Crossing his arms, he scowled. "I know you are somewhere you don't belong."

"So are you," she pointed out.

"This is my family home."

"It's your *brother's*," she said. "You're being deliberately obtuse."

"And you're being obstinate."

"*I'm* being obstinate? Me?" This was such a ridiculous argument, and yet it was familiar. They'd argued like this all the time, and he was reacting exactly as her Maxim would react, and—

Stepping forward, he deliberately loomed over her. "I come into my library to find a trespasser, poking around in *my* things."

"Waithe Hall is shut. Roxwaithe hasn't been here in years. *No one* is supposed to be here. You aren't even supposed to be *alive*. How are you even *feeding* yourself?"

Pinching the bridge of his nose, he shook his head. "Why am I arguing with you? You're a trespasser I don't know."

Rage, such as she'd never experienced before, exploded. How dare he? How dare he pretend not to know her? Her fingers curled into fists and she told herself she could not punch him. She was a lady, and he was a *clodpole*. "Don't be *stupid*."

He stilled, and something flickered in his dark eyes. "You will leave the way you came."

"With pleasure," she snapped. Pushing past him, she stalked from the library, through the entrance hall, and wrenched the door open. Rain pelted her, almost horizontal as the wind howled and lightning crashed across the sky. She plunged into it, anger propelling her even as she was drenched in moments.

She'd not gotten more than two strides before a large hand grabbed her shoulder and hauled her back inside. Maxim slammed the door shut and shook himself, water falling to the marble floor. "Do you have any brains?" he demanded.

"You told me to go. I have no desire to say here with *you*."

"You wouldn't get half a mile before you'd catch your death. You'll stay here."

"It would not be proper," she said stiffly.

He laughed harshly. "Hunting a ghost is not proper, either. You will stay here."

Mutinously, she glared at him. Damnation. She could not even *argue* that point. Belatedly, she realised the rain had plastered his shirt to his body, clinging to hard muscle and broad shoulders.

Mouth abruptly dry, her breath locked in her chest.

He didn't seem to notice her distraction. "Come," he said, holding aloft a lamp he'd magically produced, before turning on his heel to stride down the corridor. Hesitantly, she followed.

They wound through the Hall, climbing the grand stairs and making their way to the family apartments, the corridors she remembered from her—their—childhood. Wrapping her arms about herself, she cursed herself at the soaked fabric. She'd only brought two gowns, and now both were wet.

He halted before a door. "You may stay here," he said, pushing it open.

Passing him, she entered a bedchamber, again with most of the furniture covered. The bed, though, was not, holding a mattress along with pillows and sheets.

Surprise filled her. "Is this where you sleep?"

He placed the lamp on the dresser. "Goodnight."

"Good—?" He was gone before she finished the word.

Wrapping her arms about her torso, she stopped herself from rushing after him. She wanted to assure herself she hadn't imagined him, that he was real, that he was alive…and she needed to get her bag, she had a nightgown and a change of underclothes, and—Maxim was alive.

She collapsed onto the bed. The bed he had slept in, unmade with the sheets rucked to the foot of the bed. A faint scent wound about her, woodsy and indistinct, but she knew it was his, knew it was

Maxim's. A harsh sob broke from her, and another, eleven years of emotion exploding. Sliding from the bed, she pulled herself into a ball, hot forehead against her updrawn knees, her cheeks wet, her chest hurting.

The wind howled, rain pelting the window. They'd all thought him dead. *She'd* thought him dead. Her dearest companion, her best friend. Maxim.

Slowly, her sobs subsided. She couldn't stay here. She couldn't take his bed from him, and she.... She wanted to know. She wanted to know everything. Why was he here? Why hadn't he gone to his brothers? Why was he lurking in Waithe Hall alone? When had he returned?

Did he really not remember her?

Taking a shuddering breath, she wiped at her cheeks. She needed to know and surely he would tell her. Even if he didn't remember her.

Rising to her feet, she squared her shoulders. Well, she would make him remember her...and then she would make him let her hug him.

TEACH ME

by Cassandra Dean

Ever curious, Elizabeth, Viscountess Rocksley, has turned her curiosity to erotic pleasure. Three years a widow, she boldly employs the madam of a brothel for guidance but never had she expected her education to be conducted by a coldly handsome peer of the realm.

To the Earl of Malvern, the erotic tutelage of a skittish widow is little more than sport, however the woman he teaches is far from the mouse he expects. With her sly humor and insistent joy, Elizabeth obliterates all his expectations and he, unwillingly fascinated, can't prevent his fall.

Each more intrigued than they are willing to admit, Elizabeth and Malvern embark upon a tutelage that will challenge them, change them, come to mean everything to them…until a heartbreaking betrayal threatens to tear them apart forever.

SILK & SCANDAL
THE SILK SERIES, BOOK 1

by Cassandra Dean

Eight years ago...
Thomas Cartwright and Lady Nicola Fitzgibbons were friends. Over the wall separating their homes, Thomas and Nicola talked of all things – his studies to become a barrister, her frustrations with a lady's limitations.

All things end.
When her diplomat father gains a post in Hong Kong, Nicola must follow. Bored and alone, she falls into scandal. Mired in his studies of the law and aware of the need for circumspection, Thomas feels forced to sever their ties.

But now Lady Nicola is back…and she won't let him ignore her.

ROUGH DIAMOND
THE DIAMOND SERIES, BOOK 1

by Cassandra Dean

Owner of the Diamond Saloon and Theater, Alice Reynolds is astounded when a fancy Englishman offers to buy her saloon. She won't be selling her saloon to anyone, let alone a man with a pretty, empty-headed grin...but then, she reckons that grin just might be a lie, and a man of intelligence and cunning resides beneath.

Rupert Llewellyn has another purpose for offering to buy the pretty widow's saloon—the coal buried deep in land she owns. However, he never banked on her knowing eyes making him weak at the knees, or how his deception would burn upon his soul.

Each determined to outwit the other, they tantalize and tease until passion explodes. But can their desire bridge the lies told and trust broken?

About Cassandra Dean

Cassandra Dean is an award-winning author of historical and fantasy romance. She grew up daydreaming, inventing fantastical worlds and marvelous adventures. Once she learned to read (First phrase – To the Beach. True story), she was never without a book, reading of other people's fantastical worlds and marvelous adventures.

Cassandra is proud to call South Australia her home, where she regularly cheers on her AFL football team and creates her next tale.

Connect with Cassandra

cassandradean.com

facebook.com/AuthorCassandraDean

twitter.com/authorCassDean

instagram.com/authorcassdean

bookbub.com/authors/cassandra-dean

To learn about exclusive content, upcoming releases
and giveaways,
join Cassandra's mailing list:

cassandradean.com/extras/subscribe